Lumanti's Memory
/Lu: mənti:/

JENISHA MANANDHAR

Cover by: Shayashkar Dangol
Cover Image: AI Generated (Canva)
ISBN: 978-1-7635627-0-7
First Edition: 2024

A catalogue record for this book is available from the National Library of Australia

Published by Project Baakha Productions
www.projectbaakha.com

To the one and only who would be the entirety of my best memories.

Prologue

She was waiting on the platform for her train when someone tapped on her shoulder with a very well-known gesture and familiarity in their eyes, but that very familiarity was amiss on the former's eyes. It was rather met with strangeness as she kept on looking at the handsome stranger in front of her with questions, not necessarily of "What do you want" but more like, "Can I help you?"

He did not fail to notice the distant tone in her eyes and her next words shattered something deep inside him that he was trying extremely hard to keep together.

"I am sorry. Do I know you?" she said with curiosity.

He stood there in surprise when the loud noise of an incoming train echoed in the crowded platform. Suddenly he felt utterly alone standing there. She started looking sideways and towards the train that had stopped in front of her. Glancing at him one more time, she stepped onto the train while he just stood there looking at her leaving on the train that had just arrived, holding onto beautiful memories they both shared but only he remembered.

Chapter 1
A Birthday Reminder

Aaron

A name flashed on my phone screen and the ringing phone dimly illuminated the dark room of mine. It was late at night, but I was wide awake from the dream that I just had. I saw her name and jolted up from my bed immediately.

Her name flashing over my phone screen brought back many memories. Her teasing smile, her hazel eyes that always sparkled in front of me. I was incredibly surprised to have her calling me after a year, but it also worried me about what might be the reason that she was calling me in the middle of the night. Is she in trouble? Does she want me to be there for her? Is somebody else calling from her phone because something happened to her? Leaving all this quandary behind I decided to pick up the call before it ran out while my heart thumped loudly inside my chest.

I slid my thumb across the screen to pick up the call and brought my phone near to my ear, but I could not bring myself to say anything, so I just listened. The voice from the other end was calm, unlike my mind at that moment. It was heavenly to hear her voice again after all this time- after what felt like an eternity; though she had only said, "Hello." A rush of calmness came to me, and my heart fluttered upon her one hello, but I did not fail to notice that there was some sort of strangeness in her voice. I responded with the same word, Hello.

She remained silent for a while and with quiet a hesitation, she asked, "Hi, umm...is this umm... I am sorry to disturb you like this, but there was a reminder on my phone to call you right now, so I thought I should?"

I was shocked, startled and a little hurt to say the least. Was this her way to wish me Happy Birthday? Is she trying to find a reason to talk to me? I have been thinking ways to hear her voice, trying to find an excuse so I could talk to her, but her very words and our last conversation would stop me. I still remembered her words clear as day, "It is better for us to not contact each other. Talking will only make it harder." Then why was she making this initiative?

How could she do this to me on my birthday? Was this some sort of joke? Not knowing what to say I replied, "Sorry, what? Are you trying to say that you don't know why you are calling me right now?"

"I am sorry. This might feel like a joke to you, but my phone had a reminder to call you tonight. And I felt that it must have been important, so I called you maybe you know something?"

Her words took me back to my birthday a few years ago when she pretended to forget my birthday.

***

"Hey, so am I to believe that my girlfriend does not know my birthday?" I was teasing her that day for not remembering my birthday.

To which she feigned surprise and responded, "Oh my god, is it your birthday today? I didn't know. I should set a reminder on my phone." She then proceeded to spoke into her phone, "Hey Google, remind me to call Bee on 15 June every year at the midnight," then she smiled back at me, typed some more in the phone and showing her phone to me she said, "Here done." She had put the note on her calendar reminder as: "Don't forget to call, Bee. Very Important."

"Why didn't you just add it as my birthday?" I asked.

She just shrugged to my question.

"Wait, so you seriously forgot my birthday?" I pressed on.

"Well, technically I did not forget, I didn't even know. You have never told me."

I smirked at that statement. "Then whom did you order a birthday cake for?" I said showing her the receipt she had clumsily put on the kitchen counter.

***

And that was her first failed attempt at giving me a surprise birthday party. Though I would end up learning about her plan, I had always appreciated all the effort that she would put into my birthday. All that effort she would put into making me feel so special and lucky. Every year after that, she would come up with even better ideas to make it special. Her surprise plan for last year's birthday was amazing. She kept me guessing throughout and nobody spoiled it either. It would have been the perfect night if it had not been followed by what happened later that night.

I did not expect any surprises this year because she was no longer part of my life and this call in the middle of the night is as surprising as it gets. However, I would put it in a shock category rather than surprise. The most surprising was that she was not lying, and she was as clueless as she sounded making this phone call. Then it hit me like a bus that she had moved on from me. She does not even remember my birthday and the only reason she is calling me in the middle of the night is because her phone said so. How easily she forgot this day! I did not know what to say so I stated, "Umm, well, it is my birthday. I do not recall anything important."

"Oh," she chimed, "then it is an important day, Happy Birthday!!! I guess that was what that reminder was for."

"Umm Thanks, I guess." I just wanted to end this phone call but some part of me still longed to hear her voice a little bit more.

I was hurt but confused by her call and about all of this. I also felt a bit angry about why she would call me after successfully avoiding me since our break-up. Could she be drunk? But she did not sound like it. I took a deep breath before speaking, "T, I missed you terribly in the past year but right now our conversation is making me hurt all over again. So, I am sorry, I am not in a condition to talk right now or be part of whatever is going in your head."

"I am sorry to bother you. It was a mistake," she sounded a little hurt. Why did she sound hurt? I did not mean to be rude. Before I could apologize or say it was not a mistake, she hung up abruptly as if she did not want to embarrass herself or know what to say next. It was not a mistake. Though it hurt me and made me miss her more, I was still delighted to hear her voice and the effect it had on me even after all this time, I do not think I can go on without seeing her or being with her anymore.

Why did she sound sad? Why did she call me today of all the days? Why was it a mistake? Why? Why? Why?

The moment I came close to forgetting her, letting go of her, her memories kept me awake at night and now her phone call made everything even more difficult.

Was it someone else with her phone? But that could not, be I knew her voice way to well for not to recognize it. Even after a year of silence from her, her voice was always in my mind. It was her beautiful melodic voice with hint of sternness and care that made me fall in love with her. Her voice had always calmed me at the most stressful times and made my day.

Suddenly a text appeared on my phone, "Hey, I am sorry, silly me, disturbing you on your birthday. You enjoy your birthday. I hope you have a great year. Happy Birthday."

She had practically moved on if she did not remember my birthday or maybe she did but didn't want to acknowledge it. I sat there in my dark room confused, sad and yearning to hear her voice again, without thinking much, I decided to call her, but as if on cue, my phone started buzzing up with my friends calling me one after another to wish me 'Happy Birthday.' My notification tab was now filled with birthday wishes from my friends but all I wished at that point was to hear her voice.

Today, hearing from her after such a long time, it tugged something in my chest. I wanted to see her, speak to her and stare at her all day long. I did not realize that how much I had missed her until today. I thought I was over it, but my heart still longed for her presence in my life.

Chapter 2
Who is Bee?

Lumanti

There was a hint of familiarity in that voice as if I had heard that voice before somewhere. Who was this, Bee? He had this husky, yet soft voice and it seemed as if he was just waking up from a dream. I did not remember that voice at all, but I wondered if he was someone I knew. Could he also be someone I had forgotten about? But could I have forgotten such distinct sexy voice? If I had forgotten him then probably it was not an important part of memory. *Or could be the worst part of memory.*

Earlier tonight, I was scrolling through my phone watching 60second videos, this one video was talking rather passionately about *revenge bedtime procrastination*, which was probably what I was doing. Taking that video as a cue, I decided to stop my scrolling exercise. I was about to put my phone on charge when a notification pinged. It was a reminder that very specifically said,

"Don't forget to call, Bee. Very Important."

What kind of cryptic message had my old self left for the present me? I wondered. Was I supposed to find Bee in the middle of the night? Did I learn bee language to be able to call bees at night? I laughed at my own expense. That was very absurd thing for me to put a reminder for. Maybe there was something on my notes or contacts, I mused. Then I put the word Bee on my phone's search button and surprisingly a contact number appeared in the search results. The contact's name for this person, whoever he was, had name put under as Bee followed by emoticon of flying bees.

I tried to decode the message of what could be so important. Why did I need to call Bee tonight? I tried to look for messages between this person and me but there was nothing. I realised then that they could only recover my cloud data. Anything saved on my phone was unrecoverable. Now I was curious, why did I need to call this person. I knew it could wait till morning but if I had put this reminder specifically for this time then I should give it a call, I argued with myself. It must have been important. I should just do it- at least to keep my mind at ease. I would not be able to sleep if I didn't call this person.

I was nervous making this call. As the dial tone went through, each beat of that tone felt like forever. I was about to put the phone down but then I heard the tone stop and the breathing of the person on the other side, but that person never spoke, so I spoke, "Hello?"

The person whoever it was on the other side did not speak, there was a noticeable pause before he said, "Hello." Even that one word made me weak on my knees. I craved to hear more, so I initiated rather nervously, "Hi, umm...is this umm...," words were failing me, "I am sorry to disturb you like this, but there was a reminder on my phone to call you right now, so I thought I should?"

It was a nerve-wracking conversation, but also somewhat comforting at the same time. It felt like I could trust him, but it seemed I might have offended him somehow for not remembering him and his birthday. I realised it was the reminder to wish him tonight which I did not do so properly, so I texted him a short and sweet message to mend the damage, I guess.

I could not bring myself to explain to him that I didn't remember him due to my partial amnesia. I almost got scammed once when I confided my condition to someone, I thought was a friend. Luckily, Rianne, my best friend for life came to save me from that sorry existence of a person. But conversing with Bee was something else; I wonder if that is his real name.

It was almost four months since it all happened- since Rianne had to rush me to hospital. I did not remember why I was rushed to the hospital, but it was since then I had lost my memory- well partially lost my memory. Whenever I met my friends, they would tell me, "You used to be so sad, so glad you look happy now." They didn't know that all the sad memories were forgotten or rather suppressed as my therapist would like to call it. It was maybe a good thing that I didn't remember them, but I still wondered about my past and was curious as to what might have happened. Whenever I tried to put pieces of my life together, a new puzzle appeared surprising me and encouraging me more to find answers. Just like this reminder.

A text message pinged on my phone. It was a reply to my text message,

"Thank you, T. I am not sure what this call means but I am glad you called."

I am not sure either Bee. I am not sure either.

I didn't know how to respond to that message. His message felt like he was disappointed. I wanted to ask him more questions about what relationship we had and why did he sound disappointed and maybe he could have answered me more, but I didn't want to embarrass myself and give him more information. It seemed like he knew me but for me, he was practically a stranger.

***

"Hey, Ri, do you know anyone named Bee or someone I call as Bee?" I asked Rianne the next evening, who was busy preparing meals for our movie night.

"Who?" responded Rianne with surprise in her voice.

Rianne and I have been best friends since our kindy days. We have been with each other for everything that happened in our lives from our first heartbreak to our first achievement in life. Basically, we had known each other our whole lives; we could write biographies on each other's life. As my memories are bit tainted at the moment, I am not sure if my version would have correct account of our lives. But my therapist had said that I am making progress, and I would be able to regain my memory slowly. At least it was not a permanent loss. So meanwhile, I had to rely on Rianne for my memories.

She did not look at me and just started placing some frozen spring rolls and fries inside the air fryer. Since our graduation, four months ago, we had decided that we would catch up with each other weekly if possible and every month, we would catch up for movie night even though we would be living at the opposite ends of the city. It was her turn to host the movie night so there I was waiting for her to answer my questions while I nibbled on the popcorn she had prepared for us.

"Bee? Do you know him?" I pressed again because I knew from her tone of voice and this deliberate silence that she knew something.

"Why do you ask?" she questioned instead of answering my question.

"Just because... Do you know him?" I pressed on.

She shrugged and attempted to change the subject, "Should I hit up the pizza now or maybe it can wait?"

"For god's sake Rianne. Who is this, Bee? Why are you trying to avoid answering who he is?"

She sighed heavily and then she blurted out, "OK fine. He is your ex."

What?

"Oh" It was the only sound my mouth was able to make after realising that I called my ex in the middle of the night on his birthday. Gosh! He must have thought that I was trying to talk to him. He must have thought that I was crazy. I so wanted to see the face that voice belonged to. Now that he is my ex, should I even want to? What if he is handsome and he has moved on already? *He did not sound that he had moved on from his voice.* My delusion spoke. *He is ex for a reason*, my conscience chimed. He sounded so nice and sexy, I wondered why we broke up.

Then something changed in Rianne's face and the realisation struck, "Wait did you remember something? Is that why you are asking?"

I knew how my loved ones were waiting for me to regain my memories. Though thankfully it was a not a complicated amnesia, it still meant I did not remember some of the milestones of my life, some of the lessons of my life. I could not participate the same way people would remembering fond memories. I understand not all people remember everything that happened in their life but for me even recent memories like my graduation day were blurry. I did remember somethings clearly for which I was thankful. I had not forgotten all the fond memories. Though it was for good that some moments are forgotten, I would like to remember them all, good or bad because I had always believed it was the moments that made me what I am today.

I did not want to get her hopes up, so I shook my head no which triggered her next set of questions, "Then, why did you ask about him?"

"I may or may not have called him last night because of the reminder on my phone."

"What was the reminder for?"

"It just said to call him and turns out it was his birthday."

"Oh, wow it had already been a year."

"Been a year for what? What do you mean?"

"Since you guys broke up." The realisation got hold of me that I called him on the anniversary of our breakup. How cruel I must have sounded to him.

"Well technically, you broke up the day after his birthday," Rianne added as if that could make it any better. I called him and asked him basically what was so special about the day. I couldn't say anything in response, so Rianne spoke again, "Are you alright, Ray?"

"Hmm, I guess so. Why did we break up?" I asked her because ever since I heard his voice yesterday, I couldn't get rid of it from my mind. What must have happened?

"I don't know," she responded. Of all the people in the world, she should know. I told her everything, didn't I? How is she going to write my biography if she didn't even know why I broke up with my boyfriend? *Not the right time to think about it.*

"What do you mean? If you don't know then who will?" I asked frustrated.

She sympathized with me and said, "I understand it is frustrating Ray, but honestly you never told me. And before the wheels of your mind start turning in wrong direction, no it was not because we stopped sharing things with each other. It was just unfortunate timing. The day you broke up with him, I was at my family's place, going with my own issues. You texted me that you broke up. I called you but you said you didn't want to talk over phone regarding this."

"If I had broken up almost a year from now, I would have plenty of time to tell you about it, wouldn't I?"

"Yes, but you went to Nepal after that for your family's function and once you were back, you didn't want to talk about it. You seemed hurt and you genuinely wanted to avoid any conversation surrounding him. You got engrossed in the studies after that. We all thought you were doing fine and if not bringing him up would help you then we decided not to bring it up."

The *ding* sound of air fryer startled us both. I took the popcorn and set it on the coffee table. She plated the spring rolls and after putting frozen pizza into the oven, she joined me on the couch.

When I remained silent for too long, she must have thought that I was trying to remember the reason for our breakup and maybe that's why she said, "You will get the answers when it is time for you to get it. That's why you are going to those sessions remember? Don't rush to the answers that are better to come at the right time. Don't pressure yourself too much. It is not good for you."

In fact, I was not sure if I even wanted to remember the past. If I was so heartbroken that I did not even want to talk about him then it must have been a really bad break up.

"Do you think he cheated on me?" I asked. My voice was too small. She pulled me towards her by her arm making me rest my head on her shoulder when she said, "I don't not think so Ray. As far as I know Aaron, he was hopelessly in love with you, so no I don't think he cheated on you."

I didn't know if she was saying that to save me from another heartbreak or if it was really the truth.

"Lumanti Ray Jones, you are a strong woman. Don't worry about these silly memories, we will make the most out of the present ones," she said trying to lighten the mood.

"I guess, you are right."

Chapter 3
To Talk or Not to Talk

Lumanti

After our fun movie night, she insisted on me staying over claiming it was late night. I knew she wanted me to stay over to make sure I was alright after that phone call from Aaron. Aaron-what a lovely name. Thanks to Rianne slipping his name in our conversation earlier, I could finally know what his real name was. But I still wondered why he was saved as Bee on my phone. *Oh Gosh! Did I used to call him, Baby?*

Throughout the night, I contemplated if I should talk to Aaron or not. As a solution to my dilemma, I decided to do the classic social media stalk instead, though I had no memory of what he looked like.

I looked him up on every possible social media, but he seemed to not exist in any of those. I tried different variants of his name as well. It was not like there were not several Aarons on social media, there were, in fact, quite a many, but none of those Aaron felt familiar and there were not any mutual friends either and most importantly, none of those Aarons were celebrating a birthday that day. It might sound stupid, but I felt like I would know him if I saw his face. His voice felt familiar to me. I almost asked Rianne about his socials, but I knew that she would be against me looking him up on the internet. I understood what she meant but there was this nagging feeling of wanting to hear his voice again, wanting to know more about what went down. I was getting curious but there was no answer.

With the limited information, I couldn't find him on the internet at all. I mean what was I even thinking, I didn't even know his full name. There was also a possibility that he had blocked me off the social media. How childish! Or what if I had blocked him? I didn't know my past self anymore- so I had to doubt that I might have blocked him instead. So, I checked my blocked list, and there was no one on my block list sharing his name. Then I decided to make a fake account to look him up. I still couldn't find any faces that felt familiar. Maybe one of them could have been Aaron but I just couldn't recognise him. I was tempted to call him again, but I realised it would do us no good to call and talk to each other. We had broken up already and I couldn't ask him to revisit those memories with me.

***

The next day, I woke up to a nice and warm morning at Rianne's place. After I got out of the shower, I started preparing breakfast for us. Ri woke up a little while later thanked me for the breakfast and went straight to the coffeemaker.

Then I finally gave up and asked Rianne to give me his socials. I just wanted to put a face to the voice, so I told her about my last night's effort and asked her to just show me his face or give me his socials.

To my surprise, she seemed to be suppressing her smile, and then she said, "I could have saved you all the trouble of searching for him on socials."

"You mean you would have given me the details?" I asked not believing what she just said.

"No of course not. I still think seeking him is not a good idea; for him and you. It could have saved you trouble because he is not on any social media. I don't know why. He used to have them, but it seems he has sworn off the social media."

"How do you know?" I asked with scepticism not failing in my voice. For all I know she might just be saying that to prevent me from looking for him.

"You blurted it out once. You had never mentioned his name before that since your breakup. You suddenly decided to look him up on Instagram and when you didn't find him, you looked him on every other social media available. Then I think you also created a fake account to look up, but he was nowhere and then you said, "He is not even on LinkedIn." As if that's the account one must have."

"It is."

Rianne shook her head and said, "That's what you said then as well. I was about to ask you more about it that night but," she paused and with strain on her voice she added, "Later you had to be rushed to the hospital."

We both didn't speak for a while, both not wanting to reminisce that night. I had noticed earlier that she was glancing at her phone occasionally, so to deviate our topic of discussion and to diffuse my curiosity over her love life, I had to ask, "Are you waiting for Sara to respond?"

She smiled sheepishly and said, "Yes, we had been talking over Snapchat almost every day, so I thought it was high time I asked her out."

"Finally, yes, so where are you guys going?" I said excitedly. I was glad that my best friend was finally doing something about her crush on Sara.

"I am planning to take her out on a dinner then hang out by the bar in the city later."

"Sounds good, has she replied yet?"

"She hasn't. She had a late-night shift so probably she is still sleeping."

Rianne met Sara when I was in a hospital. Sara was the nurse on the floor that I was admitted to. As Rianne was visiting me frequently, she used to ask all sorts of questions to Sara and Sara would happily provide them. Later, they became good friends even after I got discharged. I knew that Rianne had a crush on her the very first time Sara came to check on me on her navy-blue nurse scrub. She was in awe for sure. She couldn't stop talking about how amazing Sara was and how great she was at her job. She would have probably asked her out then and there, but the circumstances didn't allow.

After finishing my breakfast, I kissed her on the cheek and wished her good luck for the date and I left.

While entering my apartment, I saw that there were missed calls from him. He must have called me when I was driving. I didn't call him back mostly because I didn't know what to say. I was clouded with the dilemma if I should call him back or if I should heed Ri's advice of letting the past be in past. I did realise that he ought to know that I didn't remember him so that he could move on from the call I made yesterday. I wished I could tell him the truth, but I also feared the unknown. What if the hidden memories are better the way they are? Well-hid deep inside my brain. I felt guilty for not calling him back.

Should I check my old hard drive? A thought arrived in my head as I could not let Aaron go from my mind. My therapist had advised against it because he wanted me to take it slow. He didn't want me to be overwhelmed with information. I guess he was right because my head had started to throb quite a lot. I shut down my computer and went to bed to close my eyes so that my head would stop hurting.

Chapter 4

Once upon a time

It was a serene morning with birds chirping nearby and a cool smooth breeze brushing her hair. They were sitting by the bench in front of a pathway alongside a river. It was a lovely and warm day after a cold night. They were laughing and stealing glances at each other once in a while. He looked at her like he could not ever love anyone like he loved this girl beside him. And her eyes reflected the same. It was a quiet morning with only a few people walking around. It was almost as if they had this lovely place for themselves.

"So, B, what do you want to do today?", she asked with excitement in her eyes.

"I don't know. I trust you have something up your sleeve like always," he teased her.

Every year on Aaron's birthday, Lumanti, planned a surprise party, which usually derailed in the surprise part; sometimes one of their friends would spoil the surprise while once, a receipt from cake shops on the counter revealed the idea. But it was going to be different this time around.

"Hmm, what are you talking about?" she replied to him, "I am not planning anything for you tonight. You always figure it out somehow so this year I decided no planning, no surprises. You will know what to expect." She gave her most convincing smile.

"Really?" he pouted with little pretence of hurt in his face, "I was looking forward to it."

"I thought we could go to a restaurant for a nice dinner. Just you and me."

He was confused by her reaction because he still couldn't believe that she hadn't planned anything for his birthday but then again, he also liked the idea of spending his birthday with just her, so he smiled and said, "OK then, where are we going?"

"I have booked a table for us at your favourite restaurant."

His eyebrows squinted at first trying to remember which restaurant she was talking about and then it hit him, "But it is so hard to get their booking. How did you get it?"

She smiled proudly and said, "I have my ways." She then proceeded to ask him, "Are you ok with it? I know we always celebrate it with your friends, but I thought it could be only us this time, as you know I am flying to Nepal for three months next week." That seemed to have convinced him that there was indeed no surprise this time around.

He wanted to spend more time with her as well, so he said, "I know T. It is ok. I am glad that I get to spend more time with you on my birthday. Especially now that I will get to see you only through a screen for the next three months."

"I know. I don't like the idea, but my mom wants me to go see her family and learn more about her side of the family as well you know. " She said turning her head towards him and leaning towards the back of the bench.

"But why for three months?" He asked, turning his head towards her.

"Because..."

"I know I know Janku of your grandpa and your cousin's wedding, but why is it three months?"

Lumanti was born to a mixed family with an Aussie dad and a Nepali mom and being raised in Australia she rarely got to truly witness the traditional culture of her mother's side. These functions were going to be quite an exciting chance for her to witness her culture and relish it.

Janku is the celebration of an individual's 77 years, 7 months, and 7 days on earth, in the Newar community. On that day, grandchildren, and great-grandchildren if they have, will pull the chariot with the very person on it. The Janku happens at different stages of life when reaching a particular age.

"You know I will be doing much more than just attend these functions," she said in a matter-of-fact tone.

"What do you mean?" he asked curiously.

She shifted excitedly on her seat and began, "Well, my cousins are overly excited to have me there so they have this whole list of itinerary that we will be doing when I am there. We will be doing some white-water rafting, bungee jumping, and late-night clubbing." She gave her sneaky smile as she went on about what else she would be doing there.

"Wait, What? You are going to that all without me?" he pouted.

"Didn't you also do all these things last time when you were in Nepal? You kept on travelling so much with your cousins that you hardly had time for me."

"Yeah," he agreed. He then looked away and sighed as if he remembered something distasteful from the time when he went there.

"Why? What happened? You don't want me to go?", she asked unaware of what that reaction was about.

"No. No. It's not like that. I am just going to miss you so much," he replied.

"Aww, I will miss you too," she responded pulling him into her embrace.

Later that day, Lumanti not only took Aaron out for dinner at his favourite restaurant, but she also threw an amazing birthday party for him with his friends. That night held many surprises for both Aaron and Lumanti.

Chapter 5
Revisiting Old Days

Aaron

Our memories haunted me every day and every night. I dreamt of that day again. The day when we went on a date for my birthday to my favourite restaurant. The surprise she threw for me, inviting all our friends and preparing a special video edit, made me feel like I was the luckiest man on earth. However, I only dreamt up to the part where it was all shiny and happy, making me crave those days. Even though those dreams intended to keep me safe by only showing me beautiful memories, I still remembered what that night entailed; as that special night came to a close, it brought me back to the reality that I had been running from.

Her phone call broke all the willpower I had in me to move on from her. I knew that I should move on, especially now when she sounded like she had moved on. I could not possibly make things right this time, *or maybe I can. What if I tried to make things right? But what if she had already moved on? If she had moved on, why did she call me yesterday?*

I stayed at home day sulking and waiting for her to surprise me like she used to. I was so pathetic. We had broken up why would she call me or throw me a surprise party? The phone call must have been a mistake. A sheer defeat of willpower. Maybe that's what happened. I shouldn't think much of it. I didn't call her but waited for her to call me the entire day. What a waste of a birthday! A few of my friends invited me to go out and enjoy the night but I didn't. I slept in instead. I drank a little whiskey that was in my cabinet and slept. That was the only way to not miss her or remember her. I guess I didn't want to celebrate my birthday if it was not with her.

Then, morning came, and I woke up from a dream full of her smile. These memories were killing me, but these were the only things that reminded me of the best part of my life. How truly I lived with her by my side.

If she could call me out of nowhere, breaking our word of not contacting one another, I can do it too. If she could mess with my mind, I could do the same. I was going insane, and I would blame it on my insanity for making this phone call. I dialled her number without giving much of a thought, but she did not pick up. Another call and she still didn't pick up. No response. Maybe she was at work, maybe she didn't have her phone with her, I gave the excuse. I decided to wait for her to return my call. She didn't call me at all and neither did she return my call. I stayed at home the whole day waiting for her I decided not to call her anymore and waited for her to call me back. I was glad that she didn't because I didn't know what I would say to her.

Later in the evening, Liam showed up in front of my house. I knew he was here to cheer me up because this birthday I did not have T planning things or making this special. I needed to distract myself, so I took up on his invitation to go out. We couldn't go out on my birthday because I was sulking, but I couldn't do the same thing the day after either. If not my birthday, I could be celebrating my breakup anniversary. We did some arcade games and caught up with more friends at the bar. It did help to keep my mind off her, but a tiny little part of my heart hoped maybe she would come and say surprise with poppers flying around. I was hopeless.

That little hope, however, did get a little spark when I saw her best friend in the same bar. I assumed if Rianne was here, Lumanti would be too and this all might be a ruse that T planned for my birthday. Then, that hope got deflated as quickly as it appeared because when a bloke in front of me moved, I saw that Rianne was with a girl that I had never seen her with before. A part of me wanted to go and talk to her; ask her where Lumanti was and if she knew why she called me while the sane part of me argued that Rianne might be on a date, and I should not interrupt. All that determination of not thinking about that phone call washed away just because I saw her best friend. What would happen if I saw her?

However, when I got a few drinks on my system, the sane part did not have much say. I noticed that her date had left, probably to go to the restroom, and the ladies' room always had a tremendous line (I had known it from T's relentless complaints about it), so I walked towards Rianne in the hopes of having a conversation about the only girl I cared about Lumanti.

"Hi Rianne, how are you doing?" I asked smiling at her.

Rianne looked up from her seat and seemed surprised seeing me there, then she smiled and said, "Hi Aaron, I am good. How are you? Happy Birthday!"

"Thank you. See even you remembered."

She looked at me confused and then slowly it seemed to occur to her what I meant by that. I am sure, Lumanti and Rianne had talked about T's phone call to me. Heck! They must have laughed about it as well. As the bitterness of this truth hit me, I downed the drink in my hand and put it on the counter.

"So, she told you that she called me, huh? And did you both laugh about it?" I slurred.

"No Aaron, it is not like that. Why would we do that? It is just-," she hesitated a little and added, "that she didn't realise it was your birthday when she called you."

I snorted and asked, "So she has moved on well, eh?"

She remained silent looking guilty. So, our relationship was not as important to her as it was to me.

"It was, Aaron," Rianne spoke defending her best friend, and I realised that I had spoken my thoughts out loud.

She added, "I don't know what happened between you two and why you broke up, but I think-"

"I refused to believe that you knew nothing. The kind of friendship you two share, there could be no room for secrets." I interrupted.

"You can believe what you want but we never got a chance to talk about it."

"I don't know how to feel about this. I have been going crazy for not being able to forget her all the while she had moved on happily without me. I didn't know what I expected though."

"Enough Aaron," her stern voice made me shut up immediately. There was a fierceness in what she had to say to me, "I don't know what you went through, but I have seen her having an equally hard time trying to forget you and that probably is part of the reason why she never tried to talk about you. I could see her hurting as well so you don't get to say that she had it easy."

I didn't say she had it easy but knowing she also missed me as much as I did and this break-up affected her as much as it did me, made me feel a little better. That realisation didn't make me feel any better about myself though. It was only the satisfaction of knowing that the bond we shared was important to her as well.

She seemed to be in deep thought as if contemplating over her next words.

I instead asked her, "Where is she? Why did she call me last night? Was it just because of the reminder on her phone? Or was it a ruse that she is using to not admit that she wanted to talk to me?"

She looked down at the floor and then at me, "Ok, it should not come from me, but I guess you deserve to know that Ray-" she fidgeted a little and I got nervous.

"Ray, what Rianne?" I gritted my question.

"I don't know how to say this, but she does not remember you."

I didn't know what I expected her to say but that was not it. Whatever she said did make a little sense if I were to consider the strangeness in her voice yesterday. It was the voice she used to talk to the strangers. *No, I refuse to believe it.* She hadn't forgotten me. How could she possibly forget me? Forget us?

As I could not speak any further, she rubbed her hand against my shoulder. I found my words after a while, "What do you mean she does not remember me?"

She took a deep breath and spoke again, "She is suffering from dissociative amnesia, which causes her to forget- not remember certain moments from her past. She does not remember most of the things and-"

"I am one of those things," I completed her sentence and she nodded. I asked her, my words almost a whisper, "How?"

Before she could answer, her date returned, and I knew that our conversation was over. She was not going to answer me now that her date was back. I didn't wait for the formalities of the introduction, so I walked away.

She had forgotten me. While I was tortured by our memories, she didn't even remember them. What a cruel joke! Yes, it hurts me to remember her and not have her by my side, but I could never let go of our memories, no matter how much it killed me or made me miss her. It could be the same for her too, right? I am sure it was not in her control, but it was still not fair that only one of us carried the burden of our memories. I slumped to the ground outside the bar and a lone tear escaped my eyes as I hated myself for letting her go. For not being there for her when she needed me. For not giving her the answer that she wanted to hear. For not knowing what had happened to her. For not telling her what was going on in my life. I hated it. I desperately needed to talk to her, so I picked up the phone and called her again, but she didn't pick up. This time I needed her to pick up my call. I wanted to whirl my phone out into oblivion.

I couldn't sleep the whole night. As always, her memories kept me awake.

Chapter 6
Train of Thoughts

Lumanti

My mind was in a constant state of turmoil, debating whether to return his call or continue ignoring him, as I waited for the next train to arrive at the platform, longing to go home and rest my exhausted head. The work was dreadful today and with my thoughts revolving around his phone calls from last night that I deliberately ignored, I couldn't concentrate on my work at all. It was a constant battle of picking up the phone and putting it down while contemplating dialling his number. The work was mundane today with few meetings and few advert materials to check. I was hoping to get the job in the studio soon so I could leave this place. Maybe moving away from this city with the excuse of a job might do some good for my brain.

Why did he call me so consistently? Again, my thoughts went towards him. There was no break from this nagging that my brain liked to put me up for.

I was lost in my thoughts when I felt the tap on my shoulder, bringing me back to reality. I was a bit surprised by it, but I turned back to look at the person who broke my reverie. I had never seen this person before or at least that's what my eyes believed. He had broad shoulders, a very handsome dusky face and warm brown eyes that looked at me like he knew me. He kept on looking at me to say something, but I didn't know what to say so I just responded, "Can I help you?"

His warm eyes were now filled with strangeness, shock perhaps and somewhat hurt from my reaction, (but what had I done for such a reaction?). I realised that he could be someone I knew, and I had forgotten this person.

"I am sorry. Do I know you?" I asked with curiosity.

Before I could say anything or wait for his response, the train arrived and the crowd trying to get on that train with it. He stepped aside for the crowd to pass while I stepped into the recently opened door in front of me. I looked back at him again trying to remember him or at least remember his face for now.

I looked at him for a long time as long as the passing train allowed me to see the person standing on the platform looking at the very train that passed him by. He seemed spaced out. He must have mistaken me for someone. But his face- his face felt like I had seen glimpses of it before, somewhere, maybe he could be someone I knew.

I had too much going on my head already than to think about some random stranger on a train platform. As I reached home, all I wanted to do was lie down and do nothing, but that privilege disappeared the moment I embraced adulthood. I freshened up and ran to the kitchen to prepare food for dinner and tomorrow's lunch but today I was extra tired so I decided I would rather order in than cook- *here is a perk for adults with money but no idea how to save.*

I went to lie down and took my phone out to order something, but my fingers moved over to the notification which took me to Instagram, instead, then I just tapped through my screen, mindlessly, just watching but not paying attention. I realised in the middle of the process that I was supposed to order food but before I could move from one app to another, Rianne started calling me.

"Hey Ri, What's up? How was your date last night?" I asked her as I picked up the call.

"It was amazing. She and I had a really good time. She loves surfing too, so we are going surfing next weekend," she said it all in excitement.

"You finally found your surfing buddy," I joined in on her excitement. I had never liked surfing so whenever we go to the beach early in the morning, she would surf, and I would swim. She had tried quite a few times to make me surf, but I failed so many times that I didn't feel like doing it at all.

She had suddenly gone silent and a while later she added, "Oh and I saw Aaron too at the pub later."

"You did? Did he say anything to you?" I asked getting curious.

"He was too emotional last night, and I was slightly drunk as well-" she paused.

"What did you do Ri?" I rushed my words.

"I may or may not have told him that you have amnesia."

"What?"

"He seemed very sad about you ignoring his call after you called him first after so long." Since when she started thinking about emotional wellbeing of my exes. *Was she still drunk?*

"I cannot believe you. You are the one telling me to refrain from telling people about my condition and now you are telling me that you told him yourself."

"He is not people. He is Aaron." Suddenly, my curiosity to see him peaked. What was it about him?

"But he is my ex, is he not?" I was getting angry now, but I didn't know the reason anymore.

"He deserved to know Ray," she said sympathetically.

"It was for me to decide Ri. I will talk to you later."

"Please don't be angry."

"I am not Ri, I am just- I just need to think- that's all."

Then I cut the phone call and closed my eyes. I couldn't believe she thought it would be fine to tell him. Well, yes, I was contemplating on telling him too but still. Argh! This is frustrating.

As I put down the phone, the series of stories on Instagram began to play, probably from where I had stopped earlier. Suddenly a particular picture caught my attention- it was a selfie in front of what looked like an arcade game. One of the guys was Liam, to whom that account belonged. As far as my blurred memory told me, we became friends at Uni when working on a project, we didn't talk much then but did the formality of adding each other on the gram. Sometimes I didn't know how I remembered such things in detail but don't remember significant memories like Aaron. I focused on that picture again, because it was not Liam that got my attention, it was the other guy. Where had I seen that face? Oh! It was the train station guy. So, he was Liam's friend. He must have just wanted to say hello then. Maybe he was just an acquaintance of mine, but something was tugging on my heart insisting that he might be more than the acquaintance.

He may or may not be, I couldn't think much of it. I hadn't ordered anything yet and I was getting hungry, so I ordered some food before I got distracted.

I quickly finished my dinner, took my medicine, and went to sleep. I just needed to sleep this night off to avoid further distractions.

A text message must have pinged at night, but I didn't bother checking. The text message which I would find out later in the morning was from Aaron and it would read:

How did it happen? How did you forget me?

Chapter 7
Hint of the past

He stood motionless; his eyes fixated on her as she walked out of the building with her best friend Rianne. It was the first time he had seen her, and he was awestruck just by her presence. She had long black hair then and she was dressed in a comfortable yet stylish hoodie, denim shorts, and sneakers. She was smiling over something, and that very smile captured his heart, and he probably fell head over heels in love with her at that moment.

Rianne and Lumanti had just finished their classes and were walking out of the building. It was the day when students collaborated with each other to open stalls. One sold handmade crafts, the other sold food, and some sold antique pieces or vintage clothing. It was an interesting place where people came up with different ideas for their stalls. Lumanti would always look at them, but she would usually just stroll past them because she was always in a hurry. However, on this particular day, she decided to walk towards a stall that had caught her attention - more specifically, the person behind it. Only a few people were standing and leaving. There was a handsome fellow with a charming smile behind the counter, selling honey and sharing some bee facts. Lumanti was intrigued by him. Like him, she also felt something tugging at her heart when she saw him smile, so she decided to visit his stall - something she never did before.

"Hi, how much are these for?" she asked him as she approached the mini shop. When she and her friend walked in front of him at his honeybee stall, he just fumbled and started with, "Hi, I am Bee, sorry, I am Aaron. Would you like to know some bee fact?" He then proceeded to impart information about honeybees and honey. And Lumanti being completely smitten by him just stood there listening to his presentation which she didn't ask for and also, was not the price for the honey. Rianne, on the other hand, was snickering the whole time, looking at their interaction.

Once he came to realise that he answered everything except for the question he was asked, he stopped in the mid-sentence and spoke more slowly, "No that's not what you asked, you asked for the price. And these are $10 per jar. These are all natural and there is no mixture of any kind."

He got his one hand behind his hair and looked away from her to save himself the embarrassment. She simply chuckled and putting her loose strand of hair behind her ear, asked to pack two of those jars.

After their first encounter, they never came across each other until one evening at Unibar. She contemplated quite a while before approaching him. And after several mental turmoil and creating scenarios in her head, she finally approached him.

"Hey, bee guy," she said, initiating the conversation. He smiled and stated, "You remember me." They introduced themselves again that night, and their friendship or possibly something more began.

"I am Lumanti," she said extending her hand.

"Like a memory? I am Aaron," he said shaking her hand.

"Hey, how do you know that?"

"Because I am Newar, too," he stated.

"I am mix, actually, my mom like you is Newar and my dad is Aussie, so I am half-Nepali and Half Aussie."

He nodded in understanding. She spoke again, "So, Bee, sorry Aaron-"

"It is alright, you can call me Bee. I don't mind," he said smiling at her. She was once again smitten by him and his smile.

She always had a keen interest in learning about her mom's side of culture. So, Aaron took her to most of the Nepali gatherings, restaurants or parties associated with Nepali culture. It was his reason to spend more time with her.

Lumanti started inviting Aaron and his friends to the trip that she used to plan with her friends, whether it was camping or beach day. That was her excuse to spend more time with him.

All their friends had already assumed that something was going on between them, but they were yet to admit that feelings to each other. Whenever Rianne would ask Lumanti if something was going on between her and Aaron, Lumanti would just shrug and say, "Well, he is nice, but I don't think anything is going on."

It was during the semester break when Lumanti planned a trip to go to Blue Mountains to stay over. And of course, she invited Aaron and his buddies. On the first night of the trip, they drank, played games, and partied. The next morning of the trip, Aaron and Lumanti were the only early risers, so Lumanti offered, "Do you want to go somewhere amazing?"

"Sure, where?" he asked curiously.

She took her car keys and directed him to follow her by the wave of her hand and took him to the Princes Rock Lookout. They walked further 15 minutes downhill from the lookout point to a particular spot. And once they reached that spot, they were graced by a view of a beautiful waterfall directly in front of them. It had rained last night, so the view was especially spectacular.

Aaron used to mention that the waterfalls and nature in Nepal are incomparable and how much he missed travelling through the hills of Nepal but looking at that scene in front of him, he was in awe. Of course, he would still say Nepal has it better but surprisingly he didn't say anything.

"Wow, T, this is so beautiful and calming. Thank you for bringing me here." He said looking at the waterfall and then at her. He liked being close to nature, whether it be back home or there with her. It probably also reminded him of the place he used to call home when he was little.

"Oh, don't mention it," she waved her hand. We can get to the point where the waterfall ends but it's a long hike and my legs are not in quite good shape today, otherwise, I would have taken you there, if you were keen to walk, that is. It is more beautiful up close than here. Maybe one day we can go-"

"What's wrong with your leg?" he asked now his eyes darting towards her leg, particularly concerned.

Surprised by his concern, she was moved a little and said, "It is nothing. The last time I went bushwalking with my friends, I sprained my leg muscles a little. I can still do such mini hikes, but I do not want to risk the long walks. It is getting better though." She smiled at him.

He expressed his further concern throughout their walk returning to the car. She assured him it was fine. As they were driving back to the place, they noticed a farmer's market. Aaron suggested that they should go and get something. So, they walked into the market and picked up some fruits, homemade jams, and whatnot.

As soon as they reached the place they had rented for the weekend, Rianne asked, "Where have you guys been?" Her eyes were looking at them rather sceptically.

"None of you were awake, so Aaron and I went to the lookout and farmers market." She replied innocently.

"Really?" her best friend replied, wiggling her eyebrows, and asking if something else happened. But completely ignoring her friend's reaction, Lumanti responded, "Yeah, I have got these many strawberries and also got a jam."

"Are you kidding me that's a lot of strawberries dude."

"I know but I can eat it," she then laughed a little and said, "they are so good, just as same as my dad planted in our house last summer. But B got so much other stuff as well."

Aaron stood there mesmerized looking at her and her love for strawberries while their housemates for the weekend started devouring the stuff they brought from the market. But before anybody could even touch those strawberries, Lumanti took it away out of their reach. However, she gave just enough strawberries to others and kept the rest to herself.

Rianne asked her later, "So what happened between you two? Early morning, huh?"

"What are you talking about? I just asked him if he would like to go on a drive, and he agreed so we went." Lumanti said in a very casual tone that made her friend wonder if Aaron and Lumanti were ignoring the sparks between them or was something else going on.

After they returned from the trip, everyone got busy with their part-time jobs and Uni assignments. The hangouts became infrequent, and they ran out of excuses to see each other. Lumanti went to Unibar which he frequented, to see if he was there, but he wasn't. And it was during that time Lumanti finally admitted, "I miss him. I don't know why but I want to see him."

Chapter 8
Conflicting Emotions

Aaron

Yet another day had come to completion. I didn't know if it was Monday Blues, I had too much to drink or was it the information that Rianne bestowed onto me last night, but this day had been a long one for me. The day passed by as these thoughts possessed me and the next thing, I knew it was 5 o'clock and I was standing on the train platform. There were two tracks on this platform. I stood on the left side of it. I was looking at the time for the next train when my eyes fell on someone on the right side of the platform.

She was wearing a white shirt with a black pencil skirt and carrying her coat and bag in one hand. She was exchanging her weight from one leg to another balancing on her black stilettos while waiting for the train on her side. I knew her. I noticed that she had cut her hair shorter than she usually would. She looked gorgeous in her shoulder-length dark black hair as much as she did in her long hair. I might not have seen her for a year, but I knew her. I would always know her- even in a room full of people, I would recognise her. Lumanti.

I walked towards her not worrying that my train was on its way, and I would have to wait another 30 minutes on that platform for the train to take me home. But I could wait 30 minutes; I just could not wait for another chance encounter to speak to her. I lightly tapped on her shoulder and as she turned around, my heart leaped. I searched her eyes for recognition but all it gave me was a question. Question of who I was to her. I didn't hear what she said because I could see from her eyes that she didn't recognise me at all. It was not pretend. If I had any shred of doubt on what Rianne said yesterday, it was gone. *She didn't remember me. She had truly forgotten me.* I was utterly broken to see her eyes confirming what I hoped was not correct. I had hoped that it was Rianne's drunken bluff, or I had heard it wrong.

I didn't fail to notice the distant tone in her eyes and when my brain finally processed what she said, her words shattered something deep inside me that I was trying extremely hard to keep together.

I simply stood there in shock when the loud noise of an incoming train echoed on the crowded platform. Suddenly I felt utterly alone standing there. She started looking sideways and towards the train that had stopped in front of her. Glancing at me one more time, she stepped onto the train while I just stood there looking at her leaving on the train that had just arrived, while holding onto all the beautiful memories that we both shared and only I remembered.

*****

I had to face the truth rather harshly that she had forgotten about me. I wanted to throw the vase on the table to the wall in front of me but instead, I slumped on the couch and brought my hands to my face frustrated. What was I lamenting for? It was for good; she didn't remember me. We had broken up; there was no future to our relationship, no matter what I tried. I wouldn't be able to change that now. What had changed since we broke up? Would I be able to change the future this time if I were to bring her back into my life?

I was plagued by her thoughts and desire to hear from her, what had happened when I was not in her life. I did realise it would not bring anything good but still, my mind insisted on sending her the text message: *How did it happen? How did you forget me?*

Next morning, my phone started ringing from the other side of the room. I didn't realise that I slept on the couch last night. I got up to get the phone and as I reached towards my phone, my heart stopped when I saw her name flashing on my screen. Without giving any thought to it, I picked it up immediately. I needed to talk to her.

"T? Hello?" I said hurriedly as if she would have cut the line if I didn't say hello.

She stayed silent on the line but didn't hang up and after a second, she replied, "Was it you at the train station, yesterday?"

Did she recognise me? A small ray of hope started in my heart, but I smothered it before it could give me further hope. I could never forget the strangeness in her eyes.

"Yes, it was me." I replied curtly still recovering from the wound it gave my heart. She gasped.

I didn't know what to say but I had to ask her what had happened.

"T, Rianne told me that you have- that you are."

"That I don't remember certain things?" she completed the sentence when I couldn't bring myself to.

"How, what happened?" Some part of me did not want to know the answer because I was not there for her when it all happened. I had always known that all moments were special to her. She used to say that these memories whether good or bad makes us who we are, and she would never let go of anything that made us who we are.

"Mistakes, lessons, happiness are part of those memories so you would not let it go because they made you, YOU," she told me this one day in our random conversation. And to know that she was now deprived of those memories; it hurts rather differently. What could have happened for her to go through this, my minds were making all sorts of stories.

"Umm, I don't really remember. I was at the apartment with Ri, packing up our stuff and next thing I knew I was waking up in hospital with throbbing headache. My parents were there and so was Ri. Apparently, I was unconscious for whole night and another day. They told me that I had graduated a day ago. I didn't remember it then, but now I have blurred memory of going on stage," as T told me about this, I couldn't help but berate myself for not being there for her but how could I, we were not even looking at each other at that time.

"I am so sorry T; I was not there with you." I was starting to feel guilty about that night and frustrated that I was not there for her. I brought my hand over my face and onto my eyes to hide what I was feeling.

She continued trying to assure me, "Don't worry, that night is over now, and I am fine."

"No, I should have been there, there for you. I really am sorry T,' with tears nearly escaping my eyes, "and what happened in hospital?" I asked while I feared for the answer though I knew it was only going to confirm that she had forgotten me.

"Later in hospital, after I gain consciousness, they were asking some questions and I answered them, but I couldn't answer for some. When I tried to force myself to remember it. I fainted, at first, they assumed that could be just result of shock or head trauma. The doctors insisted on doing more test and later they came up with the diagnosis that I have dissociative amnesia and it is like as if I have isolated my memories that were foul or hurting me and chosen to forget them or blocked them perhaps.

I don't remember much of last year. I have been trying to put pieces together and when reminder popped in my phone to call you, I thought I should give it a shot for a chance to put piece together even though it is calling a stranger at the middle of night."

Stranger, I never knew that one word could hurt me this much. I was out of words and couldn't comprehend what she must have gone through. I paused and said, "Do you think you will ever regain your memories? What are the doctors saying?" *Was I a foul memory to her that her mind tried to keep at bay?*

"I am going through psychotherapy, and they are positive that these memories will make its way through to me. It is just a matter of time. Meanwhile, I just wanted to let you know that I am sorry for calling you in the middle of the night. It must have been weird for you. I am sorry if I am trying to open up the closed wounds."

"I would be lying if I said I wasn't surprised, but it was still good to hear from you."

"I am glad. Ok I will let you go to whatever you were doing before."

If she had forgotten me then I should let her go. I should let her enjoy the bliss of losing those beautiful memories and the foul ones. But I was selfish, I needed to see her. I wanted to talk to her a little more. Before she could cut the call, I hurried, "How did you recognise me?"

"What?"

"You asked me if I was the person you saw at the train station. How did you guess it was me?"

"I was curious by that incident and last night I had a dream, which made me even curious."

When she finished telling me about her dream, I asked her, "You are not playing a prank on me, are you? You and Rianne both?"

"What are you saying?" I knew she was not lying because her eyes did not lie when I saw her yesterday. She could not have turned to be an actor in a year to pull that level of acting but what she told me just now and claimed was her dream made me doubt if it was all a silly prank they are pulling on me.

"The dream that you just mentioned- it was exactly the way we met."

She remained silent at the other end and then spoke, "I am not lying at all. I was not even sure if it was something from my past. I was curious of seeing you in my dream."

"Could it be possible that more you are exposed to snippets of truth, more you remember?" I asked curiously.

"It has its own risks because too much memory might overwhelm me as per my therapist."

"Maybe some memories are better forgotten," I said recalling, she didn't have to go through all the pain again.

"But there were good memories too, weren't there?" she defended.

The moments I had shared with her were the most beautiful ones of my life. I would forever treasure them.

"What if?" she asked.

"What if?" I echoed her question.

"No, I couldn't possibly ask you of it?"

"Ask me of what?" Now I needed to know.

"Help me with my memories? I am not asking you to recount those moments with me, but I thought maybe talking with you could help me gain some of the lost memories. I must sound very selfish right now."

"Not at all. I would love to help you but are you sure you would want to relive those memories? Isn't it better to let go of the memories that hurt you?"

"Would you want to forget them?" she asked pointedly.

"No," I said without hesitation because I would never trade those memories to anything, and I understood why she wanted to know what happened in the past.

"That would not be fair to you," she said when I did not speak anything after my one-word response. She then added, "I couldn't put you through it all after all this time. All I know, you could have moved on from it and we might as well have become strangers."

Again, that word slashed right through me. I was going through my own turmoil of whether I want to see her again. The answer was resounding yes. I didn't know why but I wanted to see her, talk to her like we used to. I understood that we had broken up and there was no chance for us to get back together because things hadn't changed yet. However, I still wanted to help her if it meant to just have her there in my life talking to me. I would hold no expectations from it as long as I get to not be a stranger in her life.

Maybe that's why I said what I said next, "T, I know you don't remember me, but can we not be a stranger?" It did not matter anymore if it would hurt to reminisce those memories.

"What do you reckon, we should be? Friends?" she said with humour in her voice. It was still better than being strangers.

"You had always been an amazing friend to me. I hope I was to you too. I would love to have at least friendship with you if not anything more. If you think talking to me could help you, I wouldn't mind at all."

She remained silent for a moment then she took a long breath before speaking, "Aaron, do you really think this is a good idea? We starting off as friends? Where do you think it will lead us with all that history behind us? We have practically moved on."

"No, no, you moved on by letting me go completely from your mind," I said rather sarcastically than I intended. I knew I should have moved on, but I never could.

"I didn't have a choice," she said with her voice little higher than normal, "You have no idea what it is like to not knowing things. Not knowing whom to trust."

"And you don't know what it is like to live with those memories. I still remember them and now imagine what it is like living with those memories without that one person that you shared all those beautiful memories with."

"That person does not remember them." She said in a small voice, but I could hear the frustration.

I was hurt by her words and was speechless to say anything. I do understand it was hard for her and what she went through, so I apologised.

"I am sorry. I cannot even fathom what you went through. Maybe I am being a little greedy with wanting to spend time with you because seeing you after a year, hearing you what you went through, all I want right now is to be next to you and be there for you whatever you want me to be there for."

She said rather slowly this time, "Listen Aaron, I am sorry that I don't remember things but from what you have told me so far, it will hurt us more, it will hurt you more. Don't do this to yourself."

"No, please don't say sorry. I meant every word I just said, I want to be there for you. Just tell me how can I help? I am there for you."

She remained silent for a moment then she took a long breath before speaking, "Are you sure?"

I sighed and asked, "What would you like to talk about?"

Chapter 9
Conversations

Lumanti

Why did we break up? Was the first question that came to my head when he asked me, "What would you like to talk about?"

But I couldn't bring myself to ask that question because I didn't want him to relive those memories. *What if it had been a hurtful one?* and, I didn't want to sour our first proper conversation by foul moments. I should not deliberately look for moments, rather I should let it come to me like the dream I had yesterday.

"Most of my friends call me Ray but why do you call me T?" I asked him the question that had been nagging me since that midnight call, I made on his birthday. I didn't recall anyone calling me T, so I was curious if there was any reason behind it.

"You had never asked me that before today. There was no reason at all. I just went along with the sound of letter with which your name ended. I just found it endearing on my own sort of way."

I chuckled hearing his answer. It was such a cute answer. We both laughed and, in that moment, I blurted out, "Why didn't we become friends when we broke up?" I couldn't get a moment to think before asking that question. My heart just felt like we could have become good friends if not anything serious however I did not want to bring that topic yet and yet I blurted it out.

He did not hesitate. He answered rather slowly, "Because we were too heartbroken, and I was too egoistic. I didn't see if we could be friends with all the emotions swirling around. After talking to you again, I understand now that maybe it didn't have to be this complicated and we can start off anew."

"Thank you for doing this with me. I understand it must not be easy for you."

He went silent on the other side. I couldn't comprehend that silence of his. Was it his guilty conscience or was he hurt by this whole thing?

"Can I see you?" I asked because at this time only looking at his face would help me understand what was going on in his mind. And without missing a beat, he said, "Sure, of course. Would you like to meet somewhere?"

I didn't know if it was a good idea to meet him, but I wanted to see him and talk so that I could see the reaction. I was also hoping that seeing him can help me jog my memory somehow. I was going to opt for video chat, safer than meeting in person.

"Would you like to do video chat instead?" I recommended, and he agreed.

I added video option on the phone call, and he accepted the video request from his end.

I was nervous but for some reason I was smiling at him. He looked striking in his plain black T-shirt leaning against the back of the couch. My mind did not recognise him (except for the part that he was someone that I saw at train station and dreamt of), but at the same time it felt like my eyes and my heart somehow knew this person. Seeing him up close through this phone with no distraction, he felt familiar, and I understood my own feelings- feelings that I felt but did not recognise when I saw him at the platform.

He looked delighted and at awe on the other end of the call. I unconsciously checked how I was looking like in the camera with my wavy hair little bit short from reaching my shoulder. I moved my hair a little to tug it behind my ear. I was wearing my 'devil may care' printed plain blue T-shirt and sitting on the floor resting my back to the couch. I looked at him and felt a sudden tugging at my heart as if my heart knew how to feel for this face as if my heart recognized him, but my mind refused to. We both stared at each other for a while before any one of us spoke.

And probably to end the awkwardness, he said, "It is so good to see you after such a long time. The short hair suits you."

I could feel the blush erupting on my face as he complimented me, so I thanked him looking away.

"Did you have your breakfast?" he asked next.

I nodded yes and asked him if had done his. He replied, "I haven't. I will prepare soon."

"Do you have to leave for work soon?" I asked.

"No, I don't. I am starting late today. You?"

"I am working from home today. I will have to start working in half an hr."

"So, we have half n hr for us?" He asked cocking his eyebrows. I nodded with a smile.

"Are you on any of the social media?" I asked though I knew the answer but what if the situation had changed.

"I don't," he responded. I mean who does not have one in this age and time. He must have seen the confusion in my face, so he proceeded to explain, "I used to have account in all the platforms available but after us, I deactivated them."

"If you don't mind me asking, why did you do that?"

"We had not blocked each other like an angry couple because it would have been childish. It was a mutual unspoken thing perhaps. We didn't post much but I put you on mute on all the platforms just in case so I would not see you accidentally on the feed because it hurt. I also did not have the courage to block you off. But then I would always go to your profile to see what you were doing or just to see your photo. It was not helping me towards moving on aspect so few months ago, I decided to rather deactivate all the accounts and not be bothered by this social media nonsense at all. I was also bothered by all the happy couples in it." He tried to laugh it off, but I was starting to feel sad.

"I am sorry," I apologized.

"Why?"

"Because I am still not helping with moving on aspect."

"It just means that what we had was a special thing. It should not have been easy."

"Are you seeing anyone now?" I inquired. I didn't want to jeopardize his current relationship by walking into his life uninvited.

"No not at all. I did go on a date once, but it was a mistake. It didn't mean anything if I look back at it." He said trying to be honest.

"I guess it makes sense for you to go on a date since we were not even together," I replied not knowing how to feel about it.

"Could you meet me?" he asked and then he added, "please."

"I don't know if it is a good idea."

"I know you must be worried that I am not right person to see right now as your mind has blocked me off but please give me a chance." There was a sincerity in his voice that I couldn't ignore.

Chapter 10
Hello Again

Lumanti

The heart and its impulse. A logic never stands a chance against what one's heart wants. Every logical cell in my brain was telling me that meeting him was a bad idea, but every beat of my heart was forcing me to meet him. I reasoned maybe this time we can remain friends and be in each other's life without any drama. *But how can you even begin to imagine such a friendship with a person with whom you had already said goodbye to, and you don't even remember why,* my logic argued. Some part of me didn't want to say goodbye at all as if I was falling for this person without even realising.

We had decided to meet at Farmer's market near to my place on weekend. And the weekend was here.

I didn't realise that I was smiling while reminiscing our previous conversation over and over in my head while standing in front of the mirror, wearing my plain white sundress with small green leaves scattered around. I inadvertently touched the small scar on my forehead. It was getting smaller but still was prominent- as a reminder of that dreaded night that led me to having unreliable memories. I was nervous about meeting him and even doubting at times if I should meet him at all.

After giving up on my unruly hair as always, I got up, grabbed my purse, and slipped my feet into sneakers, took car key from bowl, and went downstairs. I got into my car and drove towards farmer's market. It was a warm day of winter and there were only few people in market probably because it was still early.

I saw him standing outside his black car wearing plain white t-shirt and navy-blue pants and holding a black jacket on his hand. His beautiful eyes were hidden behind his square sunnies. His smile widened as I started moving towards him, waving my hands. He looked at me as if he was simply happy to see me after what felt like an eternity as he waved back at me, or was it just my wishful thinking?

As I arrived in front of him, he almost moved forward to hug me but stopped when I just stood there maintaining a bit of distance. "Your smile is as beautiful as it used to be," he mumbled without realising.

"Hi," I said nervously pretending to not have heard what he had just mumbled.

"Hi, how have you been?" he replied shaking his head and moving his hand across his hair.

"Not bad," I replied.

"Do you want to pick up anything in particular at market?" he asked.

"I just wanted to come and see what they have got and pick something up. If you would like to go somewhere else, that's fine too." I decided to come to the farmer's market because I had a dream of us going to one. I thought this might help to jog some memories. I hadn't had any dream after that night that could shed light on us.

"Nah, it is alright, lets pick up some strawberries, you have always liked strawberries from market than the store ones," he said looking at the market rather than me.

"Umm, yeah, I do." I agreed as we walked into the market. I couldn't help but smile at his words and the memory that I retrieved from the dream. Somehow, he mentioning it made it feel more real than seeing a part of memory in dream. Dream didn't feel like a memory at all even if it was something that had happened in the past; it didn't feel real to me but standing next to him here, makes me feel comfortable. I should be feeling strange to meet him because I had no memory of this person apart from what I had seen in the dream, but it felt more like I know this person but just didn't know how exactly.

After the briefing and few safety warnings, we were showed the way to the farm. As we were walking through the farm, he asked, "How is your new place like?"

"Umm, it is nice and cosy. I love it. I get my solitude and space," I answered.

"Is there enough space for you to dance?" His question got me off guard. Not many people knew that I used to dance and do it sometimes. I guess he was my boyfriend so he must have known. *Could we have danced together sometimes?* I imagined but shook the idea away from my head to prevent myself from blushing and answered his question, "It is not big but yeah there is enough space to move around and flaunt my basic moves. So, you know I dance as well."

"I guess, I am few of the lucky ones who knows that you love to dance."

"So, you do," I said slowly while realizing that he was someone from my past and knew a lot about me than what I knew about him. I suddenly became anxious as I found this fact rather unsettling. These emotions were coming in waves, making me blush one second and anxious the next. As if sensing, what was going on with me, he changed the subject, "I really hope we don't have to encounter any snakes like that guy mentioned here today," referring to the safety warning staff member provided to us before going to the farm.

"Don't worry, they won't be poisonous." I assured him patting on his shoulder. We both chuckled a little at that and started walking towards the area where strawberries were found. I kneeled towards the ground looking for strawberries and he joined me in the search. We got some really good strawberries and started walking towards other side of the farm. We were now walking silently, not knowing what to say next.

Suddenly, something moved between the bushes which led me to scream and jump towards him. He caught me before I could fall; without realising my hand landed on his chest, bringing us closer. We could hear each other breathing and as our eyes met, we stumbled and moved away from each other. Not knowing what to say, I just apologized.

"Are you okay?" he asked with concern in his eyes.

I just nodded and looked away.

"Aaron," I said slowly.

"Please call me B," he said to which I further added my own question, "About that I have to ask, why did you let me call you Bee?"

"Because I like it when you said that. It felt like something only you could call me. My friends call me either Ron, or sometimes just R or Aaron. My middle name starts with B, Baby ends with Bee, I like Bee and person I love came up with it so why wouldn't I be ok with it?" he said smiling but as soon as he realised what he had just said, his smile disappeared into a melancholy. And my heart clenched to see him like that.

Chapter 11
Memento

Aaron

I began to reminisce about the first time I saw her, as we talked about how I had loved the way she had been calling me ever since we met. For a moment, I dared to think that I was back with my T and the way we used to be. For a moment, I ignored the distance in her eyes that had been greeting me since we met today. Then, the realisation of the fact that I had no place in her memory, pierced through my heart.

"What does your middle name stand for?" she asked trying to change the subject probably.

Knowing what she was trying to do, I went along with it and told her it was "Bir."

"Oh, like royals?" and then she added, "Aaron. Bir" enunciating it while pausing with each word.

When she said it in that tone, I laughed a little which led her to laugh as well. Her melodic laughter that I fell in love with then and now. I just stared at her lovingly, wanting to grasp these moments with her- trying not to let it slip past my mind.

When I realised that I was staring at her for too long, I cleared my throat and began to explain, "Umm no, their surname ends with Shah and has Bikram in the middle. Mine is more like our family's middle name. Every son from my great grandparent's lineage had had this middle name but I only put the initial B and not the whole thing."

She nodded and we walked further in the farm picking up fruits. While walking, I added, "My name is Aaron B Shrestha, if you are wondering by the way." I smiled at her, and she smiled a little back- a smile that didn't quite reach her eyes.

"Isn't it ironic that my name means memory and I am the one who does not have memory of important things in my life," she expressed.

I was sad to hear her say that. I knew how she loved living in the moment, treasuring memories and capturing them in little photographs. I didn't know what the right thing would be to say so I asked, "Will it help if I show you some pictures of us together of the places we went and the food we ate."

"Sure," she said excitedly at first but suddenly her excitement faded away as it arrived. I found myself growing increasingly concerned about her wellbeing, from what she said next, "I don't know if it is a good idea. I am told not to rush into bringing out repressed memories, it might overwhelm my mind. Um, I want to see them, don't get me wrong, but I am not sure about myself."

I understood her situation, but I couldn't hide the concern I had about it, "Then let's not go there." I said and gave her a reassuring smile while squeezing her hand gently.

After we were happy with what we had collected from the farm, we walked in front of the counter and paid for our produce. We were walking towards the car park, when Lumanti suddenly exclaimed, "Oh wait, I almost forgot, I have got a gift for you."

"For me?" I asked, surprised and giddy like a small kid when she mentioned that she had got a gift for me.

"Yes, your birthday gift." I couldn't help but smile when she took out a gift-wrapped small package from her car. From the look of the gift, I was assuming it could be a book. Past T would have known that I didn't prefer reading books, but I couldn't tell her present self.

Whatever the gift might be, I was just excited to know that she remembered to get me something despite everything. I whispered, "Thanks" as I took the gift from her.

I carefully opened the package and took out a small diary with a black cover and gold imprint of leaf on top. The paper had a bit of a rough and sturdy texture which meant it was Lokta paper (popularly known as *Nepali Kaagaz*), made from recycled paper. As I turned the pages, I noticed that there was her cursive writing addressing me in the second page. I had always loved these kinds of diaries. Even when she didn't remember me, she knew exactly what to gift me. Did some part of her still remember something about me? Suddenly, it gave me hope when it shouldn't.

My heart was pounding as I saw her handwritten note on that page and not wanting to show my emotions, I decided to not read it now, "I love it T. Thank you so much. It means a lot to me. I want to read it by myself, when I am alone, if it is alright."

Lumanti nodded and said, "Sure. And you can laugh at it as well."

I replied with, "I don't think I can do that. Thank you very much for this gift. I lo... I really appreciate this," I paused and said, "I think I will go now." I wanted to spend more time with her, but my emotions were getting better of me, and I needed to be by myself to read what she had written for me.

"Thank you for today. Have a safe ride home. Text me when you reach home," she said.

"Sure, I will. Take care T." I almost moved towards to kiss her like we used to and for a moment I thought that she almost moved forward as well but we both looked away and went towards our car.

As I sat in my car looking at the diary in hand, I remembered the day, when she visited me at my place. There was a pile of diaries and notebooks in one corner. All those diaries were made up of *Nepali Kagaz.* She was curious by it. I had told her then that I loved collecting these diaries whenever I go to Nepal. I either kept them as keepsake or wrote my thoughts on them. And sometimes I would gift them to my friends. She had told me that she would get me one of these when she goes to Nepal. Could she have bought it when she went to Nepal last year? Even if we were broken up by then? I didn't know what to think so I opened the diary instead to read the note addressed to me.

I was re-reading the words written by her for me repeatedly. My eyes were teary and thoughtful. I read again,

Dear Aaron,

Wish you an incredibly Happy Birthday. May you have a great and amazing year ahead. Thank you for making time for me and coming to see me despite knowing the fact that I don't remember you. I know I don't remember much of our common past and it must be hard for you to deal with this, but I really like your idea of starting new and I would like to give it a chance. I like the idea of spending time with you. Even when my mind fails to recognize you, my heart feels like it knows you very well. Let's get to know each other better and this diary is to symbolize the clean slate like you suggested, to fill the empty pages in upcoming days. I am sorry, I am not as good at writing as you are so I will stop here. Have a great one.

-Lumanti.

I smiled looking at the note that had warmed my heart. I couldn't help but want to see more of her.

Chapter 12
Happy New Year

Few years ago, on New Years Eve, Aaron managed to get a best place with best view for NYE fireworks. Aaron took this as an excuse to spend more time with Lumanti, so he invited her and her friends and his friends to this place to celebrate New Years Eve. Songs were playing and crowd was growing. There were around 15 people there, but the apartment felt so stuffed and crowded. Aaron was always hovering around Lumanti to make sure that she was ok. Even when he was busy talking with someone else, he used to glance at her occasionally as if he couldn't take his eyes off of her.

When the first set of fireworks started at 9, all of them were either by the balcony or by the window.

After it was over, they were all back to drinking. Some went to sleep; some went home but midnight firework was still left so few of them waited it to be 12. While they were waiting, Rianne was busy talking with the same girl that brought them drinks earlier. Aaron was talking with one of his friends when there was a sudden commotion. Some random guy tried to grab Lumanti's waist but even when she was drunk by that time, she managed to slap his hand and push him away. Almost immediately, Aaron was beside her pulling her behind himself and glaring at that guy furiously. If that guy had tried to come any closer to her, there would have been serious circumstances, but the guy just raised hand and left. Then Aaron turned and asked her with so much concern in his face, "Are you alright?" In return she nodded looking at him and slowly smiled.

He smiled back and blushed looking at her. Soon enough it was midnight, and everyone were back to balcony and window to see the show. It was a beautiful sight where colourful rounds of fireworks made its show above the Sydney Harbor Bridge. It was spectacular to see all the city brighten by the rounds of fireworks and everyone shouting Happy New Year. Lumanti was jumping and smiling, clapping her hands together looking at fireworks while he was busy looking at her. He was staring at her the whole time as if she held all the fireworks he needed to see that night. As the midnight firework ended and they wished each other, 'Happy New Year,' she leaned towards him with confidence and drunkenly said, "Hey, I heard people kiss after clock strikes 12. Should we kiss?" But he politely refused, and her ego had never been so bruised in her life. He later took her to her best friend avoiding her for the night.

"Hey Ri, I think you would be able to take care of her than I can." To which Rianne asked, "what happened?"

"Nothing. I think she wants to sleep so it is better for her to be with you than any other place in this apartment."

"Thank you. That's really nice of you," she responded.

Not able to process what happened, Lumanti decided to confront him as soon as she woke up in the morning. But that courage of confronting him might have been the drunken confidence because in the morning when she saw him, all she wanted to do was to curl up somewhere and hide. At the same time, she could not get her eyes off him.

He was looking fresh and handsome in his unbuttoned white shirt, perfectly showing his ripped body. She was at loss of words when she saw him approaching towards her.

"Good morning beautiful," he said in his husky morning voice while tucking her loose hair behind her ear. She inhaled sharply as he came close to her. He smelled like cinnamon and coffee. Not knowing what to do she took a step back, pretending to find something in kitchen counter and asked trying to sound casual, acting like she didn't remember her failed attempt at kissing him, "What happened last night?"

He cocked his eyebrows and said, "You don't remember? Well, let's see it was a fun night. You were dancing and jumping around. Oh, and this dude tried to grope you, but you pushed him away so bad that he didn't dare come close to you".

"I did?" She acted surprised.

"Yep."

"Oh my god. I must have been acting crazy." She said moving her hand over her face and hoping he would not bring up the kiss.

"No not really. He deserved it."

Before he could bring it up and embarrass her, she thought she would bring it up instead and clear the air instead, so she spoke, "No, I mean the whole night, I must have been so drunk," and as to confirm her confusion, and feigning her realisation, she asked, "Did I try to kiss you?"

He smiled and said, "Umm yes but we didn't kiss, and I took you to Ri, instead." She lowered her head in embarrassment (giving her confirmation that it was not her imagination that he rejected her) but then, he brought his hand toward her chin to make her look up and said, "hey, I didn't kiss you not because I didn't want to."

"Then why didn't you?" The question blurted out of her.

He sucked in the air and said, "God knows, I wanted to. I didn't because I didn't want our first kiss to be in your drunken state or to be forgotten the next day, I wanted both of us to be sober and you to be okay with kissing me. I didn't want you to regret it."

Her heart fluttered at his words and warm smile coveted her face and so did his. He asked, "Can I kiss you now?"

Her cheeks were flushed when she nodded and leaned towards him. But before their lips could meet, Rianne decided to enter the room, which made them move slightly away from each other. "Hey guys, what's the plan?"

***

After helping to clear up the place, everyone left either for their second round of party or to home. Rianne and Lumanti went to Lumanti's family house for New Years lunch like every year. Aaron texted her to check if she would like to go out later. As she did not have any plans, she agreed to it. She was more so glad that he texted her to go out.

It would have been first time that they were meeting by themselves and for the sole reason to meet each other with no other excuses or façade. They grabbed some food from the nearby Food Truck and went to the park. As they conversed watching the sunset, it didn't take long for the stars to fill the sky. As they sat under the star embedded sky talking about their life, he gently traced her lips with his finger. Slowly he cupped his hands around her face and lean towards her. She didn't hesitate. She moved her head towards him and as the stars shone upon them, both of their lips met with one another.

Later that night, they both reached his home unable to keep their hands off each other. As they stumbled towards his bed, their body danced in same rhythm as if each knew other's move. His hand started tracing her body while she planted kiss on his chest moving towards neck and then his earlobe. And their lips met once again and several times more that night. They made love with each other for the first time that night and every touch felt equally new and familiar as they moaned and sighed.

At present, Lumanti suddenly, woke up from her dream and as she moved her hands to her face, she could feel the fresh tears in her eyes. She didn't know why her heart was feeling heavy all of a sudden. She couldn't decide if it was a dream about her past or her brain making up stories.

Chapter 13
Date Night

Lumanti

It was a beautiful memory but why can't I still picture it being real? Why did it still feel like a dream? If our relationship was as beautiful as my dream depicts it to be then why would we break up? Could it be some misunderstanding? Maybe we could work it out this time? I did not want to hear my sanity screaming at me trying to knock some sense into me. All I wanted was to have him back in my life. I wanted to remember that kiss. I wanted to kiss him right now. I no longer cared how bad it could have ended, I just needed him right now by my side.

I got up from the couch pacing around the room, rethinking the entire dream, doubting if it happened and worrying about the consequences if I were to fall in love with him again. Was I in love with him? Not yet I was not but what if I will if the memory keeps on coming? I didn't care anymore. It was frustrating not knowing things. I screamed at my indecisiveness and in the whim of things, I picked up my phone.

"Hello," he picked up my call in the first ring.

"Hello," my voice came a little cracked from screaming and crying.

"What's wrong? Are you okay?" he asked, his voice full of concern. How could he possibly know that I was not ok from a single hello?

I cleared my throat and tried to speak calmly, "Nothing's wrong." My voice still came out a little raspy from all the crying and despite my best attempt at hiding the reality, he found out, "Why are you crying T? T, please tell me what's wrong. I know from your voice that you were crying."

His concern for some reason made me even sad and my voice began to crack as soon as I spoke, "I dreamt about us again. The night of fireworks. The night after when we kissed under the stars. Did we really or was it just a dream of mine?"

For a moment, he did not speak at all.

He took a long breath before saying in a solemn tone, "It is not just a dream, it did happen." Then he paused and continued, "Isn't that the good thing, that you are remembering stuff? Why are you crying? Please don't cry."

"Because it still feels like a dream to me- not a memory that I had lived. I couldn't relate to it."

"It takes time T; you shouldn't be forcing yourself to remember things. It will come to you. The dreams are just the start," he tried to provide solace to my frustration. But I was getting impatient with these dreams, and I hated it because it felt like watching my own movie but not feeling it. I wanted to feel that happy and content with myself. This sadness and heaviness of heart feels too big and full of weight. I just wanted to feel those moments so I could maybe get out of this grief that I have been feeling ever since I woke up but no place to put it or no reason to seek why I was feeling the way I was feeling. Was it the side effect of medicine or the effect of memories I don't remember? Everybody kept on telling me how it was for good some memories did not come back but this sadness never left though memories did and I didn't know what to do with it.

"I don't know how to explain, it is just so frustrating," I said unable to form words to tell him how exactly I was feeling at that moment. I was feeling a loss of a memory that I don't remember.

"How about we go on a date?" He asked and the whole turmoil of my mind got quiet, suddenly. So quiet that I couldn't form a word.

"What?" was the only word that escaped my mouth upon his question. I had heard him loud and clear, but I didn't know how to respond to that.

"Let's go on a date," he said slowly this time, "we will see how it goes. The date-like setting might help you with the memory." Then it hit me, he was not asking for the real date, he was asking for the pretend one so it could help jog my memory. It didn't have to mean anything; he was just helping. I didn't know how to feel about it, but I agreed to it, nevertheless.

***

We had agreed to meet outside the train station where he had last seen me. That station was where I usually changed platforms to catch the train home. So, I took the train from work and instead of changing trains, I went outside to meet him. Walking towards the street where we had arranged to meet, I saw him leaning against his car door, scrolling through his phone. He looked handsome in his black pants and cream shirt. As I approached him, he looked up from his phone and smiled. Every time he smiled, something stirred in my heart, making me feel warm and fuzzy.

"You look beautiful," he said first thing when he saw me but all I was wearing was my regular work clothes- black cotton pants and a peach satin top with a black blazer. But I had to admit, I did make an effort more than usual to make sure I looked good today.

"Thank you. You look handsome yourself," I replied to which he smiled rather cutely. He said thanks and opened the door of his car for me, which caught me by surprise because I was assuming we needn't go anywhere in the car, so I asked, "I thought we were walking so I didn't bring my car."

"The place I want to take is rather special and a surprise like I mentioned in the call, so I need to take you in a car. I will drop you home safely as well, don't worry."

"No, no you don't have to. I can take the train," I insisted.

When he saw me hesitating, he then said, "I understand you are having a hard time trusting me- a stranger," he said the word stranger rather distastefully, "So, how about you tell Rianne that you are meeting me. I can send her the location as well if she wouldn't ruin the surprise. And you two already share location, so she would know where you are throughout our little date."

"No, it's not like that. You don't have to do that. Thank you for saying that though." I said appreciating his gesture.

Rianne and I had shared our locations with each other since the time we went to the music festival and had never switched it off. But we also did not regularly check where the other one was. But I did have her in speed dial so maybe it would not be big of a risk, going out with him. I calmed my mind. I felt a little bad for doubting his intentions.

He opened the door again with a smile and I smiled back at him, shaking my head in disbelief, then I got inside his car.

He must have noticed me rubbing my palms because he cranked up the AC a little to make the car warm while saying, "It is cold today, let me warm up the car."

"So, where is this surprise place, you want to take me? I would have driven there myself you know."

"Then, it wouldn't be a surprise, would it? Don't worry, it is nearby. We won't have to drive much."

We talked about our day during the car ride and later he stopped his car by the nearest street parking. While I was about to open the door, he stopped me and then reached for the handle and opened it for me. I got out of the car smiling holding his hand. For some reason, holding him by the arm and walking together came naturally to me.

"It is just around the corner." He said and took us around an old building.

The design of the building was like that of an old classic house but as we moved inside, the interior was completely revamped making it look modern and chic. It was a cosy restaurant with comfortable couches and tables while a bar lay at the end of the room, where a gorgeous curly haired girl was tending the bar. Maybe that is why men were swarming over the bar.

But we were taken further into the venue, leading us to an open space, surrounded by glass windows that held the beautiful view of ocean. We were shown to our seats and as we sat, we were given the menu. The whole vibe of the restaurant and now this view he had booked for us was breathtaking. I was in awe the entire time and I also noticed from the side of my eye that he was stealing glances at me time and again which made me blush.

He then asked, "Have you been here before?"

"Nope. Have you? Or have we?"

"No, I came with my friends last time for Sam's birthday."

"Sam?"

"You might not remember him; you only met him once."

I nodded and looked at the view. Then he further added, "Sorry, I didn't mean it because of- your- I said it as in-

"As in people usually don't remember who they had only met once. You didn't mean to say it because of my amnesia. Did I get it right?"

He looked flushed and nodded. I just smiled and said, "You don't have to walk around eggshells when talking to me. And it is a lovely restaurant, by the way. Thank you for bringing me here."

"It is, isn't it? When I first came here, I had thought, I should bring you here one day but then I realised we were not talking anymore." His face turned sour upon the realisation and looked away. Then he pretended to look at the menu as if it held all the answers to the life. Suddenly it felt like I was a rebound for my date though if it was, it would be a rebound from me. And yet I was jealous of myself- my past self, for getting a chance to spend time with this man sitting next to me. Letting go of that thought I turned to the menu in hand as well.

We placed our order after a while and our drinks came within a few minutes.

"How is your current job?" he asked trying to change the subject perhaps.

"Not at all what I expected it to be. It is fine but I want to work for media strategy and planning in screen media at a later stage, sorry, you might already know this stuff about me, and I don't want to bore you with stuff you already know."

"Firstly, I won't get bored of things you have to say. I love listening to you talk about your dreams and passion. I know how much you love the broadcast industry and I still love to hear about them. Are you applying anywhere at the moment?"

"I had applied for one company but that is in Melbourne. I know it's way away from home but it's the best one."

"Oh wow, if you get the job, will you be moving there?" he seemed rather curious.

"I think so, yeah, the change of scenario might help."

He looked away for a moment and I didn't know if it was because of something I said.

Our food arrived at the table with two side plates. He agreed with me regarding the food being tasty. We talked a little more and enjoyed our food with the view.

There were few comfortable silences and some worthwhile conversations as the sky changed its colour outside. When it was time to pay the bill, I insisted on paying but he would not let me.

"It was my idea to take you out on a date so it should be me who should pay the bill. Take me out on a date next time and I will let you pay," he said with a wink. I wanted to take up on his offer and wanted to take him out on a date. If every date was going to be this lovely, I would take him on a hundred dates and more. Plan the most amazing dates as well but I was reminded that we had broken up once and I hadn't yet dared to ask him the reason. I knew I should, but I just couldn't bring myself to ask him.

Later that night, he dropped me off at my place as he promised. On the way to my home, we talked more about our plans and future. We both somehow did not attempt to talk about the past. As I looked out onto the road lost in thoughts for a moment, I thought out loud without realising, "I wonder if I have simply forgotten some moments."

"Not forgotten just repressed. I believe it will come out in due time," he said reassuringly. It was as if someone else wanted me to remember my memories, as much as I wanted to.

"What if I have forgotten important lessons, you know?"

"We have a whole life ahead of us to make plenty of mistakes. So don't worry. You will learn more important lessons. Your gut feeling will tell you what to do even if you have forgotten it in your head." He tried to lighten the mood as he kept his gaze in front of the road. I smiled at him.

As we reached my place, he again walked out of the car to open the door for me. I walked out and thanked him for the date. I moved forward to hug him, and it felt rather warm. I wanted us to stay like that for a moment. I wanted to enjoy this moment while it lasted. When I moved away from him my heart felt a little cold and I unconsciously wrapped my blazer closer to my body in response. I was about to move towards the door when he held to my wrist ever so lightly, but he let it go as soon as I turned around and moved a little further from me, looking away. I moved his shoulder so that he would face me and when I looked at him, I could see desire dancing in his eyes, and probably he could see the same in me. I didn't know what came to me next, I just rushed towards him and the next thing we knew we were kissing.

Chapter 14
Memory Lane

Aaron

I found myself yearning to kiss her despite knowing it was not the right thing to do, maybe that is why I let her hand go as soon as I held it. But when she touched my shoulder insisting me to look towards her, I couldn't deny the fact that the yearning lay in her eyes too. When I saw the green in her eyes sparkle beneath the starlight and her body moving closer towards me, I couldn't resist. I wanted that moment to last a little longer, even though I knew it was just a fleeting impulse and something I shouldn't hold onto. I wondered whether she truly meant it or if it would even mean anything if she did.

As I drove away from her, leaving her on the porch, a harsh reality set in. I realised that I couldn't bear to let her go, this time. I loved her way too much even if she did not remember loving me. And for the first time since our conversation in the past few days, doubts started creeping into my mind about whether it was a good idea to have her back in my life at all. I was not thinking straight when I asked for the date; when I asked her to see me, to talk to me. All I wanted was to help her and remove that sadness from her eyes. I couldn't put her through all of that again. Flashes of memories came to me, and I knew deep down that it was going to be a difficult road ahead.

***

The way I talked with Lumanti during those days, still haunts me. The frustration was killing me at that time. I was mostly angry at myself those days for not being able to tell her what had happened in Nepal and how my parents were pestering me to get married as soon as I graduated. I didn't know what to say or how to say it to her. I couldn't stand facing her because I was not able to give her the same commitment that she gave to me. She had already introduced me to her family, and I knew she expected the same from me. That was the least she could expect from me, but I couldn't even do that. The way she was raised in this city and the way I was raised partially in the same city were different. It was not going to be an easy feat for me.

However, a few weeks before my birthday and that dreaded breakup, I didn't see coming, I had decided to go see my parents who had made their residence in Adelaide. I had decided to tell them then about Lumanti and convince them somehow.

I walked into the kitchen with clear intention of talking to my mother about my girlfriend. It was easier to talk to mom than dad and I was hoping that she could talk to him on my behalf. When I reached her, I noticed that she was talking with someone on the phone looking rather worried. I assumed it was the usual family drama, but I still asked her what had happened when she put down the phone.

She took a long sigh and said, "Your cousin is getting divorced. She and her husband are fighting over the custody of the child. Poor kid. I mean why couldn't they talk and sort things out instead of reaching the point of divorce," then abruptly pointing the phone in her hand towards me she said, "you see that's what happens when you don't marry someone from similar background. I knew she marrying a white guy was bad news."

While my mother continued over this family issue, I didn't dare to add to that pile. Talking with them about me and Lumanti, with this issue surrounding my mother's mind, was not going to work at all. I felt bad for my cousin. I knew it had nothing to do with the cultural differences but had to do with the rushed marriage. While I was making the mental decision to not give my opinion on this situation and not to pile on my case to her, my dad came bursting into the room asking, "It was not Reva who wanted to break it off, it was you, wasn't it?"

"What?" I said looking for my phone which later I noticed was on my father's hand.

"I just saw the notification on your phone from your girlfriend. That's why you didn't want to meet anyone." He said showing the screen of my phone towards me that showed a message from Lumanti that popped in the lock screen:

@lrjones sent a message "Hey love, I have booked ...

The rest of the message was not visible, but the first bit was sufficient for him to know that the message was from my girlfriend.

"No, if he had a girlfriend, he would have told us," My mother defended me.

"Why would he tell us? He wanted to date around instead of settling."

"No, Dad, I am not just dating around here," I raised my voice a little defending myself.

"Why would he go to see Reva if he had a girlfriend. Maybe it's a mistake," my mom added.

"Chhau kyaa ya pa swo," he said in rather loud voice in Newar language directing it towards my mother.

I may not know how to respond in the same language, but I was fully capable of understanding it and that he was blaming Mom for my behaviour. I remained quiet because anything I said was only going to fuel the anger.

My parents were furious at me when Reva called it off. She told her parents that she didn't want to move here and instead wanted to live in Nepal which was not entirely a lie. She had always wanted to do something back home. My dad, however, had found it fishy when she rejected me abruptly. He was not wrong to doubt me at that time. He kept on telling Mom that I might have done something wrong for her to reject me like that. When he saw the snippet of T's message on my phone, he found all the evidence he needed for his doubt to be the fact. He then started telling me how I can't date someone who doesn't understand our culture. How it was embarrassing for him in front of his friend when his daughter did not want to marry me. Then he went on and on about marrying someone who shared our culture and belief.

Why didn't we just stay in Nepal if he loved his culture so much? It was the thought that crossed multiple times in my head that evening, but I didn't dare to voice it. At that moment, I was so tired and mad, that I didn't even feel like giving any further explanation about my relationship with Lumanti and how important she was to me. My mom with her eyes full of stress and concern, then, looked at me and said rather firmly, "If you had a girlfriend then, why didn't you say anything to us? Why did you agree to meet Reva?"

Because Dad wouldn't listen. I would have said that, but before I could speak anything, Dad spoke instead, shutting me down, like always, "We will search for a good Nepali girl for you just like your sister found someone from Nepal. And that's final. You need to stop with your dating nonsense."

I realized that if I were to talk over my dad, it would only escalate things and impact my mom's stress levels. Despite wanting to tell him that Lumanti was not just a fling, as he assumed, I knew that it was not the right time to do so in front of my mom. The doctors had advised us that medication would help her for now, and she should avoid stress as much as possible. So, I didn't say anything and kept silent. I knew that they wouldn't listen to me that day. With that in mind, I left home sooner than I had planned.

When I came back, T was waiting for me.

I found myself torn between my desire to marry the girl beside me and my loyalty to my parents' wishes. This dilemma might seem ridiculous to someone who was born and raised in this city, but for me, it was a challenging decision. When you grow up with the idea that parents are like gods, and we should never go against them, living in a new city and spending most of the teenage years on the opposite side of the world with the very parents who brought you there, could never change that conditioning.

After the birthday date, she drove us to my place. As we walked inside, all my friends screamed "HAPPY BIRTHDAY." I was taken aback by the gesture. The place was lively with all my friends and fun she had planned for the night. I was delighted that night by the surprise she planned for me and almost forgot about the conversation I had with my parents just a few nights before. That one night held a lot of surprises for me than I expected.

After cutting the cake, I had just moved away from the crowd of friends and thanking everyone for the surprise when I got the call. It was video call request on Messenger, and I was surprised to see that it was Reva calling me.

I went to the empty room and picked up the call, "Happy Birthday!" she said from the other end as soon as I tapped the green button.

"Thank you. What a pleasant surprise!" I responded.

"I at least deserved a thank you from you for rejecting to marry you. I hope it might have helped deter your parents from talking about marriage?"

"Haha, yeah, thank you for that. They didn't believe it at first. My dad thought that I must have acted ridiculously for you to reject me." She laughed at my expense and asked, "So did you tell him about your girlfriend after?"

"I couldn't."

"What? Why?"

"Yes, why? I would love to know too," a voice that came from behind me kept me frozen in place for a moment. I didn't hear what Reva was saying when my eyes met the fury in Lumanti's eyes. She was glaring at me with eyes full of disappointment. I moved towards her, but she was quick at her steps. Without waiting to hear from Reva, I cut the call. Lumanti reached the door and stormed outside. I tried to hold her by her arms, but she jerked my hand away and said, "So, this is how I know, huh?"

"No wait." I ran towards her, "T, wait, I can explain."

"Please do." She looked at me expectantly, crossing her arms against her chest and suddenly my throat went dry, and my mind couldn't form any words.

"It was-" I was trying to speak when Adam arrived putting his arm on my shoulder and he slurred, "Here you are birthday boy. We can't have you sneaking around with your girlfriend. Sorry Ray but we got to steal him for a sec."

She just gave a forced smile while Adam pulled me out of the lounge to the place where boys were swarming around the dining table. They were playing some drinking games when Adam announced, "I have got the birthday boy, here boys." He then proceeded to say something that I didn't care enough to listen when I noticed Lumanti walking out of the house. Ignoring what they were saying, I rushed towards her, "T, wait, please don't go. Let's talk."

"We will talk tomorrow," she said out loud as she reached the driveway.

I held her by the wrist, "Please don't leave."

"We will talk love but tomorrow, okay?" she said bringing both her hands to cup my face as if trying to soothe a baby who had just thrown a tantrum after making a mess.

"We will, right?" I was pleading and she said reluctantly, "Yes, we will."

And just like that, she turned away from me and left.

***

I didn't want to remember whatever that had happened after that night. I didn't want to relive those moments again. *I am sorry T, but I can't do this anymore.* I guess it was selfish of me to do that to her, but I could no longer put on the ruse of being her friend. I could not make new memories with her in the present while our past and the fear of repeating same predicament in the future tormented me.

Chapter 15
Story of Aaron

Aaron spent most of his early childhood in a rather traditional household in Nepal with his grandparents, parents, uncle, and his elder sister. At the age of 10, his parents along with his sister who was 15 at that time decided to move to Australia permanently and settle. Though they may have moved abroad, they valued their culture and tradition dearly, especially his father. Therefore, since the early age he was instilled with the idea of being an ideal son and respecting his parents' wishes. He loved and missed his grandparents a lot and he used to talk with them every day, visit them every year which later became once in a two year and then once in a five year.

When he was little and back in Nepal, he had a crush on a girl that lived next door. Her name was Reva and was same age as his. They used to play together and go to school together. She never got to be his girlfriend as distance didn't help to flourish their friendship let alone love. He tried to visit her every time he went back to Nepal, but she started to seem distant with each visit. Later his feeling for her also slowly disappeared especially after she told him that she was dating her high school classmate. He moved on from it as it was but a mere crush.

There was also a phase of him being a rebellious teenager. He dated few girls in his high school, but they were all just a fling for both parties involved. None of the relationship, he ever got into were serious one. He dated once a foreign exchange student named Claire from US during the first semester of his Uni, but the love was short lived as their differences and opinions on certain things became more evident. When things started falling apart, Claire broke it off before returning to the US. He thought he was very heartbroken then but in retrospect, he had never been as broken as he was for not being able to be with Lumanti.

After Claire, he had sworn off from women and decided only to get serious with a girl either from Nepal or someone his parents chose. And then one fine day, this girl came in front of him asking about the honey he was selling. He could not identify exactly what was happening with his heart as he had never felt anything like it before. Slowly, she began to occupy his mind, more often than he liked to admit. His heartbeats would race, pupils dilate and always smile for no reason, whenever she was around him or even when a mere thought of her crossed his mind.

They were similar in so many ways; both grew up differently but their take on life were similar. Her smart mouth, logic, understanding of things and everything about her would keep him mesmerized. Her love for cinema, desire of storytelling, and strong determination to get what she wants inspired him to dream big and work better on himself. She was making him better by heart and mind. Slowly he realized that he was falling for her before he had any control over it. From their first conversation to their first kiss, he knew that he could spend his life with her. He made her smile and made him feel happy. He was able to be himself with her. Things were going great between Lumanti and Aaron, however they were also well aware of a looming threat of future hanging above them like a sword holding on to a light thread right above their head. The threat was of Aaron's family's expectations and how it was going to be tough for them to convince them. They tried not to think of repercussions of their strong feeling for each other at first.

They used to find excuses in words like, "It's not like we are going to get married now. There is still some time." More time they spent with each other, more the realization hit hard that if they were told to part, then none of them would handle it properly.

One gloomy day when they were walking around in Uni, Lumanti said, "What are we doing? We are deliberately walking towards the heartbreak. Isn't it better to leave sooner than hurt each other later?"

"Why would you say that? Are you not serious in this as I am?" he pouted but also added with all seriousness, "I am serious about us and yes the thought of losing you scares me, that's why I am planning to go and talk with my parents about us at least introduce you to them and give us a chance."

"Are you serious? You know what, tell them that my mom is from Nepal. Maybe that will help them change their mind, I am at least half Nepali." She said jokingly.

They laughed a little and then he just stopped and looked at her lovingly. When she gave him the questioning look, he said, "We get each other like no one ever gets us. Every conversation with you is full of life, you know. I could see myself growing and being content in life with you. Ultimately in life that's what you need, right? A person who understands you so well,"

"A companion to help you survive the Life." She completed it for him.

"I will talk with them soon. Maybe when I go see them in Tihar." He reassured her.

She simply nodded with smile. They reached near library, then he bid her goodbye with kiss on her forehead, "I will call you later. Focus on your assignment and don't get up until you are done." She agreed with smile and entered the library.

He had a genuine intention of talking with his parents about his relationship with Lumanti, but before he could do that, he received a call from his dad when walking towards the car park. He took the call while walking.

His father was asking him if he would like to go to Nepal.

He excitedly said, "Of course dad. It has been long time, are we all planning to go soon?"

"Your sister is planning to stay there this Tihar, and she misses you so I thought maybe you would like to spend your bhai tika, there instead? I will arrange ticket for you."

"That would be great. I have few assignments to submit but I could complete them before Tihar. I just need to arrange leave at my current work. Wait, what about you and mom?"

"We are not so sure, your mom is not feeling well, and she doesn't want to take a long flight at the moment so I thought at least if you could go, your sister would be happy."

His sister Meekha was working in an NGO back in Nepal after finishing her degree. She was engaged at that time with her boyfriend whom she met in Nepal. It would have been a right time as well because they could celebrate Bhai Tika (celebration of brother and sister's bond). So, he was excited to go there especially when his parents were buying him tickets for it.

He didn't realise sooner that his parents had arranged for him to meet a girl there for marriage. After all the celebrations were done, he was planning a weekend trip with his cousins. He was packing his stuff for that short trip when his father called him.

After exchanging their pleasantries, his father chose a right moment to break another news to him, "I was meaning to tell you another thing as well, as you know you are graduating soon and your sister is going to be married as well, your mother and I were thinking, it's time for us to find a girl for you as well."

"Well, I think I am capable of finding my own partner dad," he said jokingly.

And his father responded, "Really? How are you going to find a good Nepali girl by yourself? Do you have a girlfriend that we don't know of?"

"Come on dad. Seriously?"

"Yes *chhora*, my son, I am very much serious about it. In fact, I found a girl for you because you didn't."

"What??? Dad, I am still young. Why do you want me to get married so soon?" Aaron was appalled.

"Hear me out first. Let me at least tell you who she is, and this might change your mind. She is Reva."

"Reva?"

"I know you had a crush on her since you were little. I recently talked with her father. You know just catching up with an old friend and during conversation both of you came up and we thought that it would be a great chance for us to be not only be friends but also relatives. So, when you are in Nepal, go and meet her once. She has grown up to be a lovely girl."

"So that was your plan, dad? You sent me here because you want me to meet some girl."

"Not some girl. You know her. She is your childhood friend."

"We haven't talked with each other since forever."

"Just go and talk to her once. I am sure you will like her, if not its ok and she also has to like you for it go forward, right?" his dad joked and his mother from the background remarked, "Why wouldn't anybody like my handsome son?"

His heart wanted to tell Lumanti everything about it, but he felt like this would only worry her. He knew that Reva was dating someone so this might be forced onto her as well which would make this conversation much easier. At least that's what he thought. He decided to sort this thing out himself without bothering Lumanti about it.

He travelled around and a week before his departure, he met Reva. He was trying to avoid meeting her as much as possible, but the time had come, and he could not ignore it anymore.

He met her at Patan Durbar Square near the museum. She had deep brown eyes and long black hair. She had her square transparent glasses on and was wearing peach long dress paired with brown sandals. She waved from her side and took him to her favourite restaurant nearby. They ordered MO: Mo: to have there and caught up with each other's life. The friendship they lost was trying to seep in through the cracks of conversations. Reva was an aspiring architect and was graduating soon as well. Her parents were pressuring her to get married, so she decided to give it a go. To his surprise, she refused to the fact that she had any boyfriend.

Instead, she laughed and said, "I do not have any boyfriend. I want to marry someone that my parents choose for me."

"But you told me,"

"Oh, it was a high school affair. Nothing serious." He knew she was lying. It was serious for them; she was in love with him. Aaron thought to himself; *I could tell from the way she told me about him. Did they break up? but it was only few months back that I saw her with him in one of her stories.*

He confronted her about it and her face turned red with embarrassment.

She reluctantly confessed, "I am sorry. My mom told me not to mention any of it. Yes, I was still with him, but my family would never accept him because he is not Newar and neither will his family accept me, so we broke up last month. We tried talking with our family but to no avail, so we just gave up."

He was surprised to hear that. Some part of his heart thought it was wrong for them to not try hard enough but other side of his knew that this might be the fate of his love as well.

He tried to help and said, "We don't have to go ahead with it, if you don't want. See, I have girlfriend as well, so I understand."

Instead, she questioned him, "Then why are you here talking to me? Did you too try talking to your parents about your girlfriend before coming to see me..."

"Not yet. It is bit complicated at my side too," he interrupted.

"What? You haven't?", she was surprised and with regained confidence in her voice, she added, "Well, you and your family don't live here so I would think it would be less complicated for you. But I guess parents are parents no matter where you live. Wait, you are here talking to me just for the formality, isn't it?"

He nodded shamelessly and said, "I am planning to talk with them soon. I had actually hoped that you would not want to be in this marriage either."

"Well, listen, for me my parents' wishes are of utmost importance to me. If marrying someone of their choice matters to them, then I am willing to do so. I just want to see them happy."

"Even it means losing your own happiness?"

"Yes, even if it means that. I have made up my mind. I hope they would understand your perspective unlike mine. I really hope out of two of us, at least one of us gets our happy ending. I mean it, I really do." There was a hint of reluctance in her voice, but she concealed it well enough.

He was stunned by her answer and remained silent. After a while he simply said, "Thank you for saying that." Her words were echoing in his ears for a long time.

He returned to Australia and was lost in his own thoughts most of the times, not knowing what to do. He was worried that he might have to break off his relationship with Lumanti like Reva did to hers. He knew that he would be devastated if he loses her, and it would make him anxious that there was a chance of not having any serious future and how this might be unfair to Lumanti. He was in constant battle with himself inside his mind. Lumanti was worried about him and kept on asking him if he was alright.

"What happened? You seem down. Did you happen to talk to your parents about us?" she asked.

"No, you know I went to Nepal in Tihar, and they didn't come at all. I want to talk to them about it in front of them not through phone. So, I have not been able to."

"Ok, it's alright..."

"Timing has not been right yet. I will let them know, okay." He knew that he sounded frustrated, and she didn't deserve that reaction from him.

"I understand, B. Don't pressure yourself with this. We will deal with this together alright. Don't stress too much."

"Ok." He sighed.

"Is this what is stressing you out?" she asked with concern evident in her eyes.

"Nothing is stressing me out. I told you I am fine." He raised his voice in exasperation.

"Ok, you don't have to be so rude about it. I am not trying to pressure you to talk to them now. I just wanted to know if that's what is bothering you. You don't have to talk about us anytime soon alright. You take your time and can always talk to me if there is anything."

"I am sorry. I raised my voice. I don't know what's got into me."

"You seem different since your return, you sure you don't want to talk about it?"

"I will tell you T when time is right. Don't worry." But the time was never right. She stopped pressuring him with her questions, but her concern was evident. He knew that she deserved to know the truth and he needed to make things right because he was certain that he wanted to spend his life with her.

Chapter 16
What is Love?

Lumanti

I was smiling as I walked into building, reminiscing the kiss we had just shared- etching it into my memory. It felt new but so familiar on my lips and my heart. I was starting to feel something for this stranger that I am calling friend now and used to call lover. *What am I doing?*

I fumbled with the keys and walked inside my apartment expecting it to be empty but was startled by Ri, who was already there, sporting an apologetic look. Sometimes I wonder if it was a good idea to give her an extra set of keys to my apartment.

"Hey Ri, what are you doing here?" I said as I entered the room. She jumped up from the couch, where she was sitting and came running towards me and hugged me.

"Well, I just wanted to see my best friend, it has been so long. Where have you been?" she asked.

"I thought you had plans tonight that couldn't be cancelled," I replied ignoring her question and putting my bag on the table near to me.

"I still do but it is close from your place, and I thought I would check on you while I wait. So, where are you coming from looking like a beauty," she attempted asking again not trying to sound like she was prying, which was exactly what she was doing.

I noticed that she had already helped herself with the juice and snacks. I took some crisps from the open packet and put it in my mouth before replying to her. I then looked at her who was still looking at me with questions on her eyes.

"Umm from a date?" I replied to it like a question, while slumping back to the couch slowly trying to evade her reaction.

"Date?" she said almost screaming, "with whom? I assumed you were on a date when I saw your location at some fancy restaurant." So, she did check my location which made me feel safe to know that someone would look for me if I got lost. I smiled at the thought.

"Umm with Aaron." I responded to her question and her excitement deflated as soon as I said his name.

"What? Why? Do you think it is a good idea, Ray? To meet him after all this time?"

"Well, you are the one who told him about my condition." I deflected trying not to address judgement on her voice.

"Yeah, but I didn't mean for you to walk back into his life. He is your ex, for God's sake. You said so, yourself. What is he even thinking?"

"Well, he could be helpful with my memories. After talking to him I dreamt about the day we met. I don't know anything more but that is a progress, isn't it?" I also dreamt about our kiss, but I wanted to keep it to myself.

She seemed a little hopeful but then her expression became doubtful and said, "It could also be because of the therapy that you are going through. I don't know what good it will bring to both of you by going through this."

"I just want to start off as friends for as long as it goes. I know it's stupid, but I don't remember anyways so how bad it can get?"

"But he does remember. All I know is, you have already let him go once and now that he is no longer part of your memories, I am just worried that bringing him back into your life might just end you up with another heartbreak. Maybe you won't remember your past with him ever but there is a chance that history might repeat itself and you both might end up hurting each other or circumstances might tear you guys apart. What if you fall in love with him again? What if he is still in love with you?"

For some reason, her last question made me feel hopeful than worried. What if he still loved me and we could work out what we couldn't in the past. I knew Ri wouldn't agree with this, so I just said, "All I want to have right now is to be somehow close to the past that I have let go. I just want to see how it goes. If it hurts, then let it. I want to feel it. I want a closure or beginning, whatever it is that has been nagging me so much. If it doesn't work out, then I will at least have a reason to remember what went wrong this time."

Both of us remained silent for a while. Ri broke the silence again by saying, "Listen, I get it you want to give it a chance. Probably your heart still chooses him. So, I won't stop you but more so can't stop you, but think of it, is it fair to him?"

I looked at the floor guiltily. I knew it was not fair to him. Unlike me he does remember the past and why it did not work out, so he should be the one to avoid me as well.

"But he said that he wants to help me so maybe he is not affected by our closeness." I shrugged as if my own words did not just affect me.

Rianne seemed to just give up, "Well, it's up to you idiots what you want to do with your love life. I have warned you Ray. Rest is up to you but just know that I am always there for you." I nodded and then move forward to hug her. Then her phone pinged with notifications.

"Well, my plan tonight included a date. I have secured yet another date with Sara, so I need to run," she said rushing toward the door. And there I was dumbfounded by what she just said, so I responded with, "When were you going to tell me that? Who goes on a date at this time of the night?"

"Well, you make the most out of it when you are dating a nurse, her shift is over and she wants to see an open sky with stars, that's all I am going to say for now," she said while putting on her shoes and before I could ask more, she spoke, "I will tell you all about it next time we meet, ok? Take care. Bye."

And just like that she rushed out of my place. I was happy to see her finally pursuing someone who deserved her. It had been long time coming.

Rianne's words revolved around my head. I knew it was unfair to Aaron. But seeing him tugs something deep inside my heart. I could see hurt in his eyes. Also, there was some sort of longing there whenever he looked at me. It was a mixture of longingness and happiness. Was it my delusion or was he really happy to see me? I wanted to hold onto him and watch him smile as night passes by. Oh! And how beautiful was that smile- only if they had met those beautiful eyes of his. Should I not have insisted on this date night?

I started to pace around my room running through my thoughts, running away from thoughts, when suddenly I got the burst of headache and it felt like I was remembering something or was I dreaming but my eyes were open. I sat on the floor taking in the headache and the new information it brought along with it.

I was walking out of the previous place and towards the park we used to stroll in the past. I was now a spectator to my own memory.

***

The park was 15minutes on foot from where I used to live. I had decided to walk partly to blow off my steam and partly to give myself sometime to think. I had texted him right before leaving to meet me. I waited for him on the park bench thinking about what I had overheard last night while reminiscing the night we kissed for the first time in this very park.

I was not trying to be ironic when I chose this location for us to meet but I might as well be. I guess I chose this place to remind him of what we had or what we still have before any of us gave up on what we had.

He appeared after a while and the way he was out of breath, it seemed like he rushed to come here. His eyes looked tired as if he hadn't slept at all and his grey tee and black trousers looked crinkled at places as if he just took whatever pieces of clothing was in front of him when getting out of the house. He dragged his hands over his face and sat beside me on the bench. He then brought his hand to mine and held on to it. I did not stop him. I needed to hold onto him as much as he did. Both of us did not utter a single word. We just sat there looking at the small walkway and trees in front of us.

I turned towards him taking long breath and said, "Why didn't you tell me?"

His body was turned towards me, but his eyes were on the ground, trying not to meet my eyes and it got me worried about what he was going to say. He finally spoke after a moment, "I didn't know how to say. I should have told you everything from the beginning itself, but I was so happy with you that I blinded myself from the reality. I tried to explain as well, but something would come up and..."

"And it helped you with your lies or may I say your half-truth?" I interrupted him and continuing to speak, my voice rising slowly with each word, "I asked you so many times what was happening, what's wrong, talk to me but you never said a thing to me. But it seems a stranger knows more about how big this problem is than me. What was your plan exactly Aaron when you went and met other girls in Nepal? And the weird thing is, why didn't you tell me anything even when I asked you most recently. Why didn't you?"

"It was not serious. I was not going to marry her. I just did that to pacify my parents for a while."

"I don't care if it was serious or not, I deserved to know. Before you went to Nepal, before you were scared to confront your parents about us. You should have been able to tell me what was going on in your head. I was in this relationship too."

"I didn't want to worry you."

"So, if I had not overheard your conversation yesterday, you would have never told me." He stayed silent, continuing to look at the ground. He didn't agree with my statement, but he didn't disagree either.

I added, "How could you go and see other girls while I was here waiting for you? You went to another country, met her and not even once you mentioned it to me. What is going on Bee? Is this me being delusionally expecting us to last while you plan to break this off?"

"NO! I fucked up ok. I am sorry. I am sorry I didn't tell you everything to begin with," he said, finally raising his eyes from the ground and looking at me. His eyes were sincere when he spoke those words. Just like that, it again flicked back to the ground.

I gently squeezed his hand and lowering my voice I spoke, "Then, tell me."

He looked up at me with confusion in his eyes. Then I added, "Tell me everything, that had happened. What happened when you went to Nepal?"

He told me everything that had happened and how his father told him about meeting a girl for marriage only when he reached Nepal. He then explained about meeting Reva and asking her help to mend this situation. All this time, I nodded in understanding.

Though I got to know what had happened, it still didn't change the fact that he hid things from me. I understood the complication of it all, but he should have been able to tell me what was going on. I looked away from him and to the sky as this conversation was getting exhausted for both of us.

"It was not only your battle for you to fight alone. You put me in the sideline deprived me of everything that was happening with you to make things work out for us. It was unfair to you and to me. We were in this together until the day you decided to carry all the burden on your shoulder. Why wasn't I part of it?" I asked.

To this he responded, "It was not my intention to hide things from you or make you feel like you are not part of this."

I interrupted, "Do you realise how it makes me feel that you were able to share our troubles with somebody else but me? If you can't trust me to be there for you when you need me the most, what am I doing in this relationship with you? We were supposed to deal with this together."

Chapter 17
Is it a Goodbye?

Lumanti

A tiny droplet of water fell on my face from above. The dark clouds above were not resisting anymore and was ready to fall heavily upon us. I had not expected it to rain so soon.

Before there could be a downpour, Aaron suggested to move our discussion to his car which I reluctantly agreed. Aaron opened his car's passenger door for me and got into driver's seat after. He quickly turned on the AC to keep us warm.

Instead of starting his car, he turned his body towards me, but I just stared at the rain splattering on the windscreen.

Before he could say anything, I said in a rather harsh tone than I intended, "So, you just decided that I wasn't good enough for your family." There was certain level of comfort now, that made me able to be angry with him and speak frankly about what was in my head.

"No, Lumanti, you would be the best person. You are the most amazing person I know."

"I am sorry, when we were dating, you knew from the beginning that you would go with the decision of your parents.," I said ignoring what he just said.

"At beginning, we were not serious about the future," he paused and said, "until we were."

"And that scared you." I said in my sarcastic tone. He did not deny it to my surprise.

"Yes, I was scared but not because of the future with you. I feared the implications of my choices."

"So, what is this? If we had tried and it didn't work out, then perhaps it would have felt more tolerable, but I found you many times not even trying."

"I will talk to them soon. I am just waiting for the right time."

When would the right time be? I wanted to scream at him. I was not asking him to marry me but knowing ultimately, we would have to end this, somewhere in the future was hurting me and him as well I assume. Why were we waiting for the torturous ending?

Then after a moment he added, his voice low, "I went home last week to tell them about us, but my cousin was getting divorced, my dad saw your message and before I could tell them more about us, I noticed my mom stressing out. She had not been feeling well for quite a while now, so I decided to not speak anything and just left home." That was why he seemed down yesterday morning and I felt a little bad for being angry at him.

"I am sorry, I didn't know that she was unwell," I said sympathising with him and at the same time I realised that he never told me anything that was bothering him. *Why does he do that?*

I then added slowly, calmer than I had been since we met, "You know, I always believed in companionship, one should be able to share both happiness and sorrow with one another. There should always be a space for every emotion. It may not be perfect in equation but there should at least be a level of commitment and vulnerability associated to it, but you were even scared to admit our love to your family or invite me to your reality. Loving someone shouldn't be this hard."

"I am sorry to have you put through this despite trying my best to prevent you from it."

"No. You don't understand B. Coming to me with your problem should have been natural to you. You didn't have to do this on your own. It required us to go through all these incidents, miscommunication for you to be able to share your fears honestly with me. We are meant to be vulnerable in love."

The clouds were rumbling and there were few flashes of lightning as the rain fell heavily above us and into the windscreen. We were safe inside the parked car for now from the weather outside but the confrontations inside was more discomforting. It felt like a silence before an intense storm. He looked hurt by my words. He just turned his key in the ignition and drove his car outside of the place it was parked. He drove silently for a while and took a turn at nearby drive thru. He spoke into the microphone and ordered for some burger, fries, and latte for two even when I insisted on being not hungry. He made the payment and drove towards other side to get the food. After thanking the server, he drove again while handing me the bag of food. I took the bags from him unconsciously, probably out of habit.

He said, "Please eat something. I know you haven't eaten anything, and I also know you are annoyed and frustrated, but you still need to eat, ok?"

He then sighed and added, "I don't want to end this. I don't want to lose you. Doesn't this hurt you? Because it hurts me," he confessed.

"It hurts me too," I stammered.

"What would you have done if I had told you everything early on?" he asked.

I finally turned towards him to talk while he focused on the road ahead aimlessly.

"I would have promised to help us out of this situation like I always said I would. I would like us to fight for what we have too. And if it didn't work out then we would have to come in terms with the bitter reality and mutually end this. We could still fight for us Aaron," I sighed and turned my gaze again towards the road.

"Do you really love me?" He asked. When I looked at him confused, he added, "I mean, even after all this. Do you?"

"I do. I love you so much." I took out a packet of fries from the paper bag and took the fries to his mouth to feed him. He took a bite, slightly turning his head away from the road but looked back to road again. I ate the remaining half of the bite. A tear slipped from his eyes, and I wiped it out and kept my hand a little while longer in his cheek as I spoke, "B, but sometimes love is not enough. Your parents have always been a priority to you. I don't want you regretting your decision of choosing me. You fear us and what it holds."

"What is that supposed to mean?"

"You are letting many fears in your head to rule you. Just take a step back and think what you want, what you need and what is right. Don't let others define it for you. If something were to happen in future, I don't want us to blame each other for the failure; I don't want you to blame me for your broken relationship with your parents every time we have any disagreements. I wouldn't want us to nurse a bitter relationship. And it is not only about this looming future anymore. Do you really think you loved me or idea of being with me?"

He expressed, "I know that I did a mistake, but I would be more open from now on. I will not hide anything from you. We will face whatever it is together. I love you. I love you so much, you know that, right?" His eyes were filled with tears now, but he was not letting it fall while I did the same.

"I have never doubted your love for me."

The rain had stopped for a while, but the darkness was at the corner as the sun bid goodbye and stars started to come out and play. As we were driving without any destination, I asked him if he could take us to my place.

The confrontations were draining us and slowly silence took over. As we reached outside the building where I resided at that time, both of us got out of the car. There were yellow streetlights shining brightly on the street.

He held my hand and said looking into my eyes, "I love you Lumanti."

"And I love you too, my love. I will keep on loving you, but love doesn't seem to be enough for us, does it? How much of back and forth are we willing to do before we realise that we are not meant to be."

"I don't believe that. We are meant to be T. We are. It was my fault, everything."

"And mine too for dragging along for such a long time despite knowing the fact..."

"No. No. No. Please don't say anything", he tightened his grip on my hands as he didn't want to hear what I was about to say.

"B, listen to me please."

He let go of my hand and turned his back against me, pressing his hand over his ears, he said, "No I can't,"

I called him putting my hand over his shoulder urging him to turn around. I tried to hug him, then he turned to face me and wrapped me tightly around his arms close to his heart while repeating his chants of "No." Tears were falling relentlessly from his eyes. He was vulnerable in front of me and crying his heart out in fear of losing me. It broke my heart to see him like that.

I kept on hugging him to calm his anxious mind and after a prolonged embrace, we let go of each other and stared into each other's eyes. I wiped the tears from his eyes while he wiped mine away.

He didn't say anything just looked at me with mixture of love and hurt in his eyes.

I said again, "I am glad you shared everything with me today. I will never be able to love anyone like I loved you, but I want you to be able to take responsibility for the decision that you make in life. I don't want to be your regret."

"You would never be. I will talk to my parents tonight about us." He finally spoke.

I rubbed his arm while saying, "I am going inside now. Please go home and think about it. I will always be at the other end listening to you. Give yourself some time and give me some time. I promise I won't go anywhere. I will be a call away. Think about it clearly as I await your decision. Promise me you will drive safe and let me know when you reach home, okay?"

He nodded with agreement and took out the brown paper bag from his car to give it to me and said, "And you better finish eating all this food, okay?"

"I will." I forced a smile.

He was about to get into his car when I turned him around to face me and before we knew my lips were on his and both of us were kissing passionately under the recently cleared star lit sky. We kissed like it was the end of the world; too scared to see tomorrow, too much in love to let go. We broke off the kiss and without saying anything I went inside the building towards my apartment with tears threatening to flood out of my eyes.

Chapter 18
Worst Nightmare

A tear came out of her eyes endlessly as she drove on the highway with no destination. The tears were streaming down her face refusing to stop. Their recent conversations were on repeat inside her mind like a broken radio. She was getting frustrated, angry, annoyed at herself. Cursing against the howling wind while hitting the steering wheel with her palm. The lights were flashing from the fast-moving vehicle ahead and she was rushing through the traffic to reach nowhere in particular- just to find a silence that she was craving for. There were several street warnings indicating the road was slippery due to the heavy rain, but she was driving stubbornly not heeding to the warning signs.

Her whole body was shaking as she was crying and sobbing through the pain. The sky was clear now unlike her mind. She played music loudly over the car stereo trying to numb all the voices and words hurting her. She sped up the car over the limit. She was drowning in pain and the words of song playing in the radio made her hurt even more.

The trees were swaying back and forth by the road. The wind was howling, and the noise of busy traffic was deafening. She took another turn and put the accelerator on full speed and rushed the car. Before she realized what happened, a shining light from the truck brightened her surrounding and hit her car from the side leading it to somersault on the road.

Lumanti's face could be seen from the upside-down car, but she was not moving at all. The road was soon filled with the blood, and she was now lying on the floor gasping for breath while calling his name. He stared at her in utter confusion unable to move but just stare at her lying body, unable to help. He just stood by the road in his white shirt with stains of red while sirens wailed in the background. She stared at him with her empty hazel eyes begging for his help. He just stared at her, helplessly. He wanted to help her and run towards her, but his feet were planted to the ground unable to move and soon the noise of sirens were replaced by the sharp ringing of his phone, buzzing in his ear like an annoying bee.

Aaron gasped and breathed heavily as he came back to the reality. His forehead was filled with beads of sweat. He relaxed a little when he realised it was just the dream- a nightmare would be more fitting word for it. He then came to terms of where he was. He must have fallen asleep on the couch after relentless pacing on the floor with dilemma shrouding in his head. He needed to talk to her, so he looked for his phone and then he noticed that his phone was continuously ringing beside him- it was the same call that woke him up. His heart felt a little deflated when it was not Lumanti who called him; it was Rianne instead. He was still not being able to identify what is real and what is not. Before he could pick up the call, the call ran out.

Why was Rianne calling me? She never calls me. Did something really happen to Lumanti? He thought. His thoughts were going to the dark places and before it engulfed him, he called back Rianne immediately, but she didn't pick up.

He got up from the couch and moved towards kitchen to get some water. He then started checking every possible website if there had really been any accident. There had been minor mishaps on the road but to his relief, none of them were on the way to her home or anywhere near her normal dwellings. Still his heart was beating faster, and he was getting anxious thinking of consequences. He called Rianne again, but she didn't pick up. He called Lumanti next, but she didn't pick up the call either. His heart was thumping loudly and his concern for Lumanti's wellbeing was increasing with each beat. He got up from his seat, grabbing his jacket and car keys, he moved towards the door.

He got into the car and rushed towards Lumanti's place while dialling her number. She was still not picking up and it didn't help ease Aaron's mind at all. Still reeling from the nightmare he woke up from, he decided to pace his mind and drive carefully so that he could reach Lumanti and make sure that she was fine. The road was fairly empty for it being middle of the night.

He tried calling Rianne again. After what felt like an eternity, she finally picked up and he sighed in relief.

"Hi Aaron," Her voice was calm but strained. Aaron's recently calmed nerve was back at being anxious.

"Rianne," he rushed, "Is T alright?"

"How did you know? Do you know what happened?" Rianne asked sounding surprise.

"What do you mean?" But he couldn't hear anything from the other end of the line. So, he shouted through the phone, "Rianne? What do you mean?"

Then Rianne rushed out her words, "She is fine now. She seems to be fine now."

"What is that supposed to mean?"

Chapter 19
A Dreadful Night

Aaron

Her laughter, her silence, her mischief, and her leaving; she was the best thing ever happened to me, but the life had different plans and we had to be apart for world didn't agree with us. The prejudice and reluctance of my family forced us to part our ways despite the love we shared. She no longer lived in her previous place but the road to her new place was the same one- just a little further down. Driving through this road all over again, it reminded me of that dreadful night- the night I was driving away from this road.

The night before we decided to end things between us. We had kissed under the streetlight, outside her previous place- unaware of the fact that it might as well have been our goodbye kiss. I had promised her that night that I will convince my parents. I had left her place with lots of thoughts in my mind, the conversations of entire day and evening reeling through my mind, driving me insane. The sky was clear, and the road was fairly empty. People must had been staying indoors with their loved ones in that wintry weather while I chose to take a longer route to avoid going to my empty house and the memories it held. The tears were streaming down my face while I drove down the highway reminiscing the kiss we had shared. The memories with her were flashing in front of my eyes.

When I finally reached home, I texted her, *Hey. I just reached home. Take care.*

Putting my phone back to the pocket, I fumbled with the keys at the front door. I entered inside my dark home not caring enough to switch on the lights. I felt closer to the darkness as I lied down on the couch trying to listen to my own voice suppressed in the chaos of voices inside my mind.

As I immersed myself into my thoughts, fighting off all the voices, I ended up asking myself, *does she deserve someone like me? She should be with someone far better than me.*

I was sad, angry, and mad then. I slammed into my bedroom door, jumped into my bed, then got up, threw everything on my side table and kicked everything that came on my way. Then I moved outside to the lounge because my bedroom was suffocating me. I kicked the coffee table and down came all the mess on top of it. I needed to unleash my anger and frustration on something. I was holding onto my hair and sobbing when I heard a door unlocking from outside. I raised my eyes and saw my dad looking for the switch in the dark room.

"Dad? What are you doing here?", I said trying to recompose myself while failing at it and quickly wiped away my tears. When dad switched on the light, the room was devastated with stuff lying all over the place, victim of my anger.

"Well, we were-" he paused mid-sentence when he saw the situation of the house, "What happened here? Are you okay?" my dad asked full of concern.

"I am fine dad, it's nothing." I stated.

"What's wrong? Talk to me Aaron. What happened here? Did someone attack you?", my father asked more sternly now.

I remained silent, not knowing what to say, I looked for Mom, but she was nowhere to be seen, so I said, "You said, we?"

"Ya, Meekha is coming, what happened here? Did *you* do all this?" he said looking at the condition of room. I nodded guiltily.

Meekha entered into the hallway addressing the noise across the street, "I guess it's yet another false alarm," and as she entered, she noticed my condition and rushed towards me, "Oh my god, what happened?"

"This is about a girl, isn't it?" dad added rather harshly.

"Maybe," I replied while Meekha stood in shock, not knowing what to do.

"You can't let a girl ruin you like this. You must be strong."

Baffled by his judgement, I defended Lumanti, "She didn't ruin me. She never could."

"Is it the same girl that I saw the text of?"

"Ya, she is the one. In fact, she is *The One*, dad. If I tell you that I love this girl so much that I cannot be without her, will you let me be with her?" I pleaded.

"No, I don't think so. Look what this girl has done to you." His answer did not surprise me, but it didn't mean that it didn't hurt.

"What if I tell you, it is not the girl but everyone except her that led me to this. You led me to this." I had never talked to my dad like that, but my adrenaline pulsing through my veins were giving me a different level of confidence that I had never garnered enough to talk to my father like that.

"So, I made you do this? Listen to yourself speaking to me like that. I didn't raise you to be like this," he responded back with his own voice high this time.

"Yes, I am listening to myself finally, thanks to her."

"She left you, didn't she? Looking at you like this because of her, it seems it was for good."

"How many times do I have to tell you, it is not because of her. Why are you so bitter?" and I went on, "Why do you have to think the worst? Why can't you for once listen to me?"

"Dad stop," Meekha shouted as I came to terms that my sister had been there all along while listening to us.

My father's hand was up in the air, ready to slap me for saying what I just said but Meekha's word stopped it from hitting me. At this moment, the noise of street was muted by the sounds of siren. It was a good thing that it was only Meekha who had seen this scene unfold. If mom had been- then I realised that mom was nowhere to be seen. Where was she? Did she even come in?

"Where is mom?" I finally asked.

Then my father spoke slowly, "She is in hospital."

"What? Why didn't you tell me that first?" I felt like I had been pushed from the cliff with nothing to hold on to as I tried to soak in the information, he had just told me.

"Because you wanted me to listen to you."

"Why are you here? Why are you not with mom?" I said with frustration ignoring his sarcasm.

"Because the hospital wouldn't let us stay till late" Meekha answered while our dad went to sit by the chair defeated with his hand on his head.

"What's wrong with mom?" I asked looking at Meekha.

Meekha took me to the other room and made me sit before talking, "She is fine. She will be fine. It is a minor surgery of heart."

"What?"

"Shshh, she will be fine," it sounded more like she needed to hear it than me.

"She will be fine," I said squeezing my sister's hand gently and to settle our hearts, I tried talking about something else, "When did you come back from Nepal?"

"We wanted to surprise you on your birthday. I landed yesterday and was planning to pick them at airport before coming here but the flight got cancelled. I stayed at the hotel because we didn't want to ruin your surprise. I went to pick them up today but once she was out of the airport, she started to feel unwell, and we rushed her to the hospital."

She put her head on my shoulder and let her tears flow before saying, "I am sorry for how dad reacted to you. I am sorry I couldn't be there for you to help fight your battles."

"It is not your fault."

"Do you want me to talk to them?"

"It's alright, it's over. Mom is in hospital, probably because of me."

"Don't you dare say that. It is not your fault; do you hear me? It has nothing to do with you. She will be fine."

Seeing my mother in hospital made me realise what Reva meant. I would also sacrifice my own happiness for my parents.

I decided that this could not wait anymore so I called her.

"Hey, what's wrong?" I couldn't help but notice the worry and pain in her voice. It sounded coarse from all the crying, and it was rushed as if something bad happened to her. I also knew for some part of it, I was responsible.

She calmed herself down and spoke slowly, "Yes. I am good. I just had a worst nightmare. You are okay, right?"

I felt like saying I just survived one of many, but I didn't say anything except, "Yes I am fine, T."

"I am glad to hear your voice," she said from the other end.

"Don't get used to it," I responded getting up from the seat and moving towards an empty hallway.

"What do you mean?"

"I mean what is the purpose of getting used to hearing my voice when it might not be for long that we will be talking, right?" I should not have said that but I was losing my mind so I further added, "Didn't you tell me that you would be ok with any answer that I bring to you."

"No, I wouldn't be ok with you telling me that we must stop seeing each other but I would have to be if that's what is best for both of us. And I also said that because some part of me was hoping that answer would be in our favor."

"Well, no T. This is not a fantasy world that you create on screen for fun, this is real life and here answer could be anything."

"I am sorry B. I know it's hard for both of us. You are just angry at the situation."

"You know what T; we created something that shouldn't have existed. I am sorry. I am sorry I didn't tell you everything to begin with. I should have made things clear with you from the beginning that it was not going anywhere, and we should have just never gotten any closer." I regretted it the moment those words slipped out of my mouth.

"You don't mean that." I hated to hear her voice so small and so hurtful. Yes, I didn't mean that, but I knew what needed to be done. The pain it had caused both of us to realise this.

"I think I do." I lied.

"Don't say that." Her voice was breaking now.

"Don't you think so? You are the one who said that love shouldn't hurt this much."

"Are you saying that this is it for us?"

"My parents will always be the priority. I am sorry."

Both of us remained silent on each side of the phone call, as if we were silently mourning the loss of the relationship that we shared. After what felt like an eternity, she spoke, "I understand. I will accept your decision. I am sorry to say this, but I think it is better for us to not contact each other. Talking will only make it hard."

I agreed silently to that. We decided mutually, I guess, not to block each other on anything but still the phone call never came or went.

I curled up into a ball and cried relentlessly that night.

I just wanted that dreadful night to end but I was also afraid to face what morning held.

My mother became healthy as ever since that surgery and we were more than happy of her recovery. They sorted out what had happened to her heart and most of her past problems were also cured.

I never saw Lumanti after that day until graduation, she looked gorgeous, but her eyes didn't twinkle as they used to. She looked away abruptly and I hated that feeling. I felt guilty again for not being able to do anything to make her smile and let those eyes shine bright. Maybe someday someone will bring that smile back and suddenly the thought of her being with someone else felt like a punch to the gut.

As I was once again driving this road towards her rather than away from her, I hoped that this night would not turn out to be a dreadful one. I hoped that I see the light at the end of the tunnel.

Chapter 20
Are you Ok?

Rianne

After my date with Sara, I decided to stay over at Lumanti's place because her place was nearer than mine. Our date nights had not yet progressed to *'your place or mine?'* situation yet. If it had been any other time or any other person, it would have happened but with Sara, I wanted to take time. I didn't want to jeopardize this. Also, she probably needed to rest after her 12-hour shift. I just wanted to take her to see the stars from the best view possible when she mentioned she wanted to see them. I prepared a mini picnic for us to sit on the hill and enjoy stargazing. I had a wonderful time looking at her and of course the stars.

When I walked into Ray's apartment, I was all cheery and excited to tell her everything.

"Oh my god! Ray, I have so much to tell you. I know I said I would tell you next time we meet. Well, I guess this is the next time. I decided not to drive all the way to my place right now." I was going on without even waiting for her to respond while taking off my shoes and walked in, "What are you doing on the floor? Are you having a cramp or something?" I asked nonchalantly thinking she was just being dramatic about our previous conversation. I failed to notice how her eyes looked weirdly open and still at first.

I was about to go to the kitchen to grab some water, when I noticed that she was not moving at all. Then I rushed to her side, "Ray, hey, what's wrong? What happened?" I checked her pulse, and she was breathing but rather erratically.

I didn't know what came on to me, instead of calling emergency, I called Aaron, assuming he would know what happened, but he didn't pick up. I then called Sara, "I am so sorry, I know you must be resting but Lumanti is acting really weird, and I don't know what to do."

In return, she asked me a bunch of questions and I answered them one by one explaining how she was curled up in the floor. Her heartbeat was erratic, and eyes were darting from one end to the other, but she was not looking at anything in particular- at least not what was in the room. At the same time Aaron was calling me on the other line. When I did not pick up, he started calling Lumanti, but I needed to get instructions from Sara before I could explain him the situation, so I ignored his call and focused on Sara's voice.

Sara was great, she explained to me calmly, "Rianne, I need you to relax now ok, Hun. From her history and what we know so far, I think she is probably having a flashback or flood of memories so just tell her that she is safe and explain your surroundings. Don't touch her but talk to her gently and firmly."

I followed her instructions, putting her on speaker and then turning towards Lumanti, I gently said, "Hey, Ray, this is Rianne, we are in your apartment. It is just you and me here. You are safe here. It has been a while since we graduated, and you landed a job too. Oh, and you remember I had told you earlier that I had a date today, remember? It was the most amazing date. Do you want to hear about it? Sara is also on the other line of the call. Hey Ray, can you hear me?" My own voice was breaking apart and Sara quickly said, "You are doing a great job love."

Ray started moving ever so slightly from her earlier frozen position and her eyes started to flicker a little. "I think she is moving."

"That's good. That's good. Continue talking to her." Sara said from the other end, and I realized that it was getting late.

"You should rest as well. If anything happens, I will call the emergency." I told her.

"You can call me anytime if you need help, ok? Or I can come right now if you need me," she responded back and I was grateful for those words but I didn't want her to trouble herself with this, especially when she herself had a hectic long day, so I told her the same and she put down the phone but not before me telling that I could call her anytime and adding further, "And by the way I had the most amazing time with you as well." I couldn't help but smile at those words.

I moved my attention back to Lumanti. I spoke further words of reassurance to her, and she seemed to relax a little. I moved towards her slowly and noticed that she was sweating profusely but her heartbeat was getting under control.

Aaron was calling continuously, so I picked it up to give it a rest, "Hi Aaron."

"Rianne," he rushed, "Is T alright?"

"How did you know? Do you know what happened?" I asked wondering if they had talked about something for it to trigger her memories.

Lumanti seemed to be still reeling from the episode. She hadn't spoken a single word, but her eyes were finally acting normal. I brought my hand to her forehead checking for any signs of fever.

"Rianne? What do you mean?" Aaron almost shouted from the other end of the call, which made me realize that he was still on the phone.

"She, she is fine now. She seems to be fine now." I rushed out my words.

"What is that supposed to mean?"

"She was having a flashback attack."

"What?"

"She looks feverish at the moment but doing better than what she was like when I had found her."

"I will be there soon." He said and cut the call.

Lumanti was now sitting upright hugging me and crying. I didn't know what to say because Sara had strictly told me not to ask her for details of flashback or pry information because that might make her spiral. So, I kept my mouth shut about it and just told her, "I am right here, if you want to talk about it."

Right then, Aaron ran into the apartment hurriedly kicking off his shoes.

He looked distressed; his hair was disheveled as if it had been pulled apart in every direction. He then slumped to the ground looking at her. He tried to move forward to her, but I slightly raised my hand and moved my head sideways to tell him to not advance as we didn't how she would react. I slowly tried to let go of her from the embrace and said, "Hey, Ray, Aaron is here. Do you want to talk to him?" She raised her head and looked in his direction while he looked at her with his eyes pleading.

"Bee?" Ray spoke slowly after a moment, her voice very small. That was the first word she had spoken in a while and I sighed in relief, at least that's progress.

"I am right here T." he said looking with concern at her tear-stained face and moving a little closer to where she was.

"I am so sorry to put you through this," then she cried again.

"Why would you say that? Please don't say that." He came a little forward and asked, "Is it ok if I come closer?"

She only nodded and he moved to sit next to her while I moved slightly away from them. When it looked like they were doing ok, I went to the kitchen to get some water.

She put her head on his shoulder and spoke, "We should talk, right?" to which Aaron responded, "No, we don't have to. Not right now. You must rest. Would it be alright, if I carry you to your bedroom so you can rest?"

She nodded again, then Aaron came a little bit closer, scooped her in his arm as if she weighed nothing and bringing her closer to him at the same attempt, he took her to the bedroom and gently kissed her forehead as he put her on the bed. I got them both some water to drink.

After drinking the water, she said, "I think I will rest a little, is that ok?"

"Of course," both of us said. She rested her head on the pillow and closed her eyes.

We left the door to her room a little ajar so we could check on her or hear her if everything was fine with her.

"It is a two-bedroom apartment. You can take the room, I will take the couch," I told Aaron directing him towards the room.

"No, I can keep an eye on her. You can go rest in the bedroom," he responded.

"I am not sleepy or tired, but you seem like you need a rest."

"I would rather stay awake. And I couldn't possibly let you sleep in the couch while I take the bedroom just to remain awake there."

He and I had never talked much even when he and Ray were dating, so, I didn't know what to say to him for what he had just said. I just shrugged to avoid making this conversation awkward and said, "Fine then, do you want to eat something? There must be something she has stuffed up in the kitchen. Help yourself."

I was about to move to the other room when he asked, "Rianne, if you don't mind me asking, what had happened? How did it happen?"

"I am not sure. I had met her earlier in the evening when she was returning from a date with you. We had a talk, and I went to see Sara."

"Sara?"

"She is someone I am dating. You would have seen her last time I met you at the pub, but you left quite abruptly. Anyway, I was not planning to return here, but I was in no mood to drive all the way to my place so I thought I will just come to see her as it had been a while since we had caught up with each other but instead I found her curled up in the floor."

The image sent shivers down my spine while his face turned pale at the thought and concern clouded his eyes. *He really did love her then why did they break up?*

"Thank God, you decided to come and see her." He spoke.

"Yeah, that thought scared me too." That was the first time on this night, I had felt the weight of what had happened. I slumped to the ground with the thought, and I felt tears flowing through my eyes. I brought my hands to my face, and I didn't even realize that I was crying.

He sat next to me on the floor and brought his arms around my shoulder, moving his hand up and down to calm me.

"How are you feeling?" He asked gently and somehow that question warmed my heart.

"I am doing fine, now that she is getting better. I just got the scare of lifetime looking at her but more scared at the thought what would have happened if I had gone home instead."

"But you didn't. You are here now, and she is fine." He reassured me. For the first time I saw him for him rather than as Ray's boyfriend who always used to linger around her. He truly was a genuinely kind person, and I could see why Lumanti was head over heels for him.

"You look equally disheveled. That reminds me how were you so sure something happened to her before I even told you?" I asked him.

"I had a nightmare. I know it does not mean anything, but I was just waking up from it and you had never called me before tonight, so I just asked in response to my nightmare and to the fact that you were calling me. I was not expecting to see her in this condition at all."

"Oh, her eyes were so eerily still when I first walked in. By the time you reached her, she was getting stable. And still, it is better than seeing her all bloodied that night."

"About that, how did it happen?"

"It was the day after graduation. We were at Uni accommodation clearing up our stuff. She was particularly sad that day with all the changes that were happening around her or maybe because she saw you at the ceremony the day before."

***

She was on the verge of depression those days. The day she casually informed us of their breakup, as though it were inconsequential, was shocking to most of our friends and her family members. Yet, it was evident to me that their separation weighed heavily on her, despite her attempts to downplay it. I knew it was hard for her, I had seen her spaced out every once in a while, lost in a memory. I tried asking if she was ok and if she wanted to talk about it, but she would brush it off like she had just let go of a fling.

After they broke up and in between the days leading to Graduation, she went to Nepal immersing herself in family functions. Once she returned, she threw herself into assignments and coursework, avoiding confronting her emotions. She didn't process her emotions at all, and when she saw him on graduation day, it might have been all it took for her to unleash those suppressed feelings. While others, including her family, assumed she was coping well, I observed her detachment and moments of distraction. Although we initially presumed their split was temporary, it became apparent that it was permanent.

She was particularly sad the day we were saying goodbye to our old apartment. It must have felt like the end of an era for her with so many things coming to an end. In that empty apartment, I could see the result of all the emotions flooding out that she had carefully hidden. She cried her heart out in her drunken mess, and I tried my best to console her. She kept on saying that she was sad because we were leaving this apartment- while that might have been true in some part, I also knew that most of her sadness was because of seeing him the day before and not being able to talk to him.

The empty bottles of alcohol were strewn across the floor as defeated as my friend. I went to get some water for her from the kitchen so that she could hydrate. While I was in the kitchen, I also grabbed some leftover chips and noodles that we had abandoned eating in the middle. I popped them into the microwave and with a bottle of water in my hand I went towards where Ray was sitting earlier. To my surprise, she was not where I had left her. I went to check in the bathroom, but she was not there either. Then, it got me worried. *Where did she go?*

I moved to the balcony and searched the entire apartment, but she was nowhere to be found. I went outside the apartment and saw her walking down the stairs very slowly and very wobbly. To my relief, she sat on one of the stairs leaning against the wall. I went towards her trying not to startle her and sat next to her.

"You know, you are the only constant in my life. You wouldn't leave me, will you?" she asked, and it broke my heart.

"Of course not," I reassured her, adding, "We are the end game, no matter how many lovers come and go. We will be the best friends for life."

She brought her pinky finger next to mine tangling them together like we used to do as kids. A lone tear left my eyes wanting to end this depression for her. I hated Aaron sincerely at that time though I had no idea why they broke up, but I couldn't help but make him the reason for her suffering. I would have called him and given him a piece of my mind that night but the events that followed didn't give me a chance to.

We got up to go back to clearing our apartment, our feet wobbly with all the alcohol in the system. As we tried to balance our feet, it got more imbalanced, and we tumbled down the stairs, half scared and half giggling. She was still laughing but all the humor was ripped away from my face when I saw blood trickling through her forehead. She said rather loudly through her giggles, "Haha, that was so funny, eh?" Her voice slurred at the end. I was trying to hold her to help her stand up but then her whole body crashed into mine and I realized that she had fainted and probably concussed. I frantically called 000 and let them know about the incident. They arrived almost immediately, and we went to the hospital. It was the longest night of my life.

Her family rushed to the hospital as well. After two days, she regained consciousness with no memory of the incident or recent events. While her memory gradually returned, some distinct pieces of memories did not make it. The doctors advised us that the memory loss was induced due to the combination of alcohol and head injury. They advised that regular therapy could help with regaining memories but also recommended taking it slow. At that moment, we were primarily relieved that she was physically well, without realizing the extent of the emotional toll it took.

Chapter 21
Memory Flood

She was experiencing a flood of memories that were safely isolated in her mind as if she was being attacked by every possible memory that she managed to secure in the back of her head with no intentions of addressing them at all. It was as if something had found the key and unlocked all the doors, releasing all of the memories at once into her mind. Her mind couldn't handle all the onslaught that came at her without any defence from her side. It was as if the memory were taking turns in taunting her. She remained frozen in front of the world while each memory came in front of her one by one with no control of her own. She let it all in giving up on protecting herself from it; accepting them as each passed by.

She was waking up in a hospital all confused and scared, where doctors were asking questions- the questions they ask when one has a neurological issue, questions like name, birthday, etc. but then they started asking some incident about her past she didn't seem to recall at all.

Then, another memory struck with the phone call from Aaron breaking them apart. The sound of Aaron's voice was so broken, and she knew he didn't want to say what he said. Then Aaron's face changed into somebody else- his face blurry, the words not clear. All the jumbled-up memories appearing in front of her with no context suddenly stopped and slowly it caught the pace and gradually, one after another memory slipped from her amygdala to her conscience.

It started with the childhood memory- it was the time when she fell from a bicycle tumbling all the way downhill. She had to take bed rest for a whole week and had to cast her right arm. This led her to fall behind on her school assignments and her dance lessons.

Then another set of memories made its way, her first crush, her disappointment at things, her teenage years and her first heartbreak. Teenage Lumanti was lying on her bed in her pink pyjama set, crying while talking with Rianne over the phone.

"I just can't believe it Ri; he dumped me. He told me that we should start seeing other people," she said.

"Ah! The nerves, what did you say?" Ri expressed her anger.

Lumanti wiped her tears and while sobbing, she said, "I said no of course but then he said he cannot do this anymore and here I was thinking I am in love with him."

"Don't be stupid. He does not deserve you. You deserve someone much better than him."

"I know but I really thought he was the one."

"Seriously Ray, we are just kids, now. There is a life ahead of us. Do you think that one guy could have been the one? You will meet more cool people in the coming days, and you will find that special one okay. Don't fret over it."

"I think I will never love anyone again."

"You will change your mind when we go to Uni. For now, let's go grab some ice cream and we can go to the beach for a swim. You need to get out of your room and get some fresh air."

They giggled and the memory took to the day when Rianne got her first heartbreak right after their high school graduation. This time Rianne was crying and Lumanti was hugging her and consoling her. Rianne was feeling extremely low and heartbroken when her first love decided to bail on her- she didn't expect her then-girlfriend to completely ignore her existence. She had left Rianne alone in the middle of the road and Lumanti drove to get her from that place.

"I am so sorry that she did that to you, but I know that your someone special is just around the corner," Lumanti said to console her.

"I guess you are right. Let's see where life takes me."

"Hey, remember, you said that we will meet more cool people in Uni to date. We will surely meet someone."

Rianne smiled she kissed her on the cheek thanked her for being such a nice friend and also said, "I am glad, we are getting out of this town. New faces, new people, new friends, here we come."

And just like that, Aaron made his way towards her mind from the memory jungle.

Then few other memories made themselves known in front of her. She remembered the times when they sang their favourite songs together in a car, danced in his house, played charades with friends, and simply laughed and gazed deeply into each other's eyes as they fell for each other. But this beautiful memory was abruptly replaced by the memory of their first fight.

"I don't get it what's your problem with that? Yes, he is my ex-boyfriend, but he is also my friend. You are very aware of that. Why are you acting weird?" she said in a rather loud voice.

"Then why do you think I am acting weird? What are we T? What is it between us?" he asked frustrated- not knowing where he stood in her life.

"Why don't you tell me?" she asked with equal annoyance.

"I don't want to be your fling. The guy you hang out with," he said, and it finally clicked in her mind that he wanted the same thing as her.

She explained slowly, "You are not my fling. What made you think that? You know, you are more than that."

"What is it then?"

Both of them were silent and then he spoke again, "I love you, T. I want us to have a proper relationship."

Lumanti was delighted to hear those words coming out of him and there was their first I love you right after their first fight.

She responded with, "So do I B. I love you too, I love you so much."

He carried her by the waist in happiness and went round and round. They both were very happy. Like every relationship, they also had their share of squabbles, but with each problem they would come out even stronger. And then he had to go to Nepal for a month. Due to time differences and network errors time and again, they had a hard time communicating with each other, but they surpassed that as well. When he returned, he brought her all the things she had asked for, but he was always somewhat lost in thoughts since his return, but he kept on saying that it was nothing. Since his return, they started getting into arguments and some arguments were never resolved. Aaron seemed more withdrawn, so Lumanti kept on asking if something was troubling him, but her concerns and questions were left unanswered with simple answers like, "T, it is nothing alright. Nothing is going on. I will tell you if there is something that you need to know. I love you." Just like that, she stopped pressing him. Things were starting to get different but their commitment to each other was still intact.

Then, the foul memory erupted from the darkest corner of her mind- the phone call she overheard, their argument and his dreadful call came through, "My parents will always be my priority." What could she say to that rather than letting him go and let him choose what was best for him and his family? She shattered on the floor and cried her eyes out that night.

She found herself now walking down the streets of *Jhochhen* when she saw the diary that he loved to collect, something that reminded him of his homeland. She bought it on impulse to give it to him when she got back home; forgetting for a moment that she would not be able to because they had decided never to see each other again. She cried again that night to sleep. It was still easy being with cousins and family there. One tends to forget their pain when they are surrounded by loving people. During that time, she either deleted or archived the photos she had with him on her phone and her socials. Being in a new city and busying herself with the family functions, the emotions did not seem to torture her as much.

Once she returned, every place she went reminded her of him. All her favourite places held their memory, and this slowly started to affect her mind, making her sad all the time, losing her interest in everything. Her eyes appeared lost or dead most of the time. She was grieving the loss of a relationship almost every day. Rianne had tried to ask her several times about what had happened, but she just couldn't bring herself to do that because telling her would mean retrieving those damned conversations again.

Soon as it was the day of graduation, and they were all adorned in their regalia, taking pictures with their family. She was taking photos with her family when she saw him doing the same with his family and all she could do was look at that family with adoration instead of wrath. It was the family that made him and brought him into her life. Despite the pain it brought her, she had a chance at those beautiful memories because of him.

All the courage she held; all the emotions she had suppressed could no longer be withheld as if seeing him was enough to break the wall that she had built so hard in the past months. It begged to come out, the tears were prickling her eyes, but she refused to let them fall because she couldn't cry in front of her family on the happy day. She looked away from him and his adorable family.

The day after graduation, she, and Rianne, were at Uni accommodation to move their stuff. As they shifted through the items and packed them up, she was overcome with sadness. It was probably because of the change that was happening in her life. She was sad to leave this place because it held so many memories. Rianne and Lumanti had shared that space since the beginning of their Uni- they had had so much fun in it. Aaron had spent so many nights there, then suddenly she started crying relentlessly this time. Once she allowed a set of tears, the flood of tears followed that she had no control of. Rianne rushed to her when she heard Lumanti wailing,

"What's wrong?"

"I am going to miss this place so much."

"How much did you have to drink?" Rianne asked.

Both of their gazes followed to the floor where all the empty soju bottles lay. They had moved most of the items during the daytime and they were just there to pick up the last item and say goodbye to the place. So, for last night's sake, they had brought in drinks and takeaways. Lumanti had just drank and drank and drank without realising, in order to numb the pain in her chest, so her emotions might have been heightened because of those nasty empty bottles lying on the floor. And it all happened when

Rianne went to pick up the call, which was, in her defense, extremely long, and she was extremely lonely.

"Oh, you poor thing," Rianne said and hugged her. She cried a little more. Then Rianne moved to the kitchen to get some water. Lumanti got up from where she was sitting and decided to get some fresh air but instead of going to the balcony, she moved out of the apartment to go to the Uni grounds which was nearby. She wanted to walk there a little more to reminisce about her time there. The stairs appeared like they were moving on their own when she stepped on them. When she couldn't take more steps, she just sat on one of the stairs and leaned on the wall. Rianne showed up and sat next to her.

Rianne's assuring words were reaching her ears when the last pieces of memory were coming to her mind. Her eyes fluttered and she started blinking rapidly, as the final memory of her falling down the stairs, the fear-stricken face of her best friend rushing to her aid, came to a close. She felt breathless and as she blinked more, she realised that she was in her apartment- not where she fell, not where she held memories of the torturous past. She was safe and in her apartment with her best friend who held the same fear and worry in her eyes as the final memory, she just came out of. She went for a hug and started crying overwhelmed with all the emotions.

After slowly recovering more from her stature, she noticed that Aaron was on the floor looking at her who was equally dishevelled and relieved. She wondered for how long he must have been sitting there. He seemed to be scared that he could break her, and she could not help but feel fragile because of it.

His soft voice made her melt. Her recovered memories and their recent encounter ached something deep in her heart that made her apologise for putting him through this.

Once Aaron put her on the bed, she closed her eyes but as soon as she was left alone in the room to rest, she let her tears flow relentlessly remembering and addressing the memories that she had just got out of.

Chapter 22
Fight for love!

Aaron

It tortured my heart to see her like that- to see her as if she just gave up on life. The very person who showed me how to live could not possibly be this lifeless. I couldn't help but blame myself for it but this time I was not running away. I would stay by her side and make sure to bring that life back to her. I would bring the joy back to her life whether she would accept me back in her life or not. I was willing to stay on the sideline and help her if that was what she asked of me.

I was blind not to see how I could have prevented it all from happening. I wanted to give this love a second chance it deserved; I could not keep on losing her. If she accepted me after all this time, I would put my best foot forward and give my best to us. I had seen that love in her eyes even if she had forgotten me- though it was dimmer than it used to be, but I would make it brighter than ever- for her, for us.

I could not get a blink of sleep as I lay down on her couch looking up at the white ceiling. I glanced at her from a slightly ajar door, the moonlight shining upon her. She looked like an angel.

Then, I heard a slight sniffle, and I don't know what came over me. My feet, as if they had a mind of its own, led me towards her door. Concern swelled in my heart as I heard her sobbing quietly, trying her best to ensure that nobody would hear. She must have sensed my presence in the room because she quickly turned around but not before wiping her tears away.

"Aaron" she spoke, her voice nearly broken. I went towards her but before I could reach her, she asked me to close the door and I complied. "Are you alright?" I asked her. She only nodded.

"I am right here if you need me. I am here to listen to you if you want to talk about it. It must be hard and overwhelming with all these memories piling on you."

"It is," she did not deny and just with those two words acknowledging the situation, her tears burst out and she wept leaning against my shoulder. Hearing her cry like that felt as if someone had put thousands of little pins around my heart. My heart was shattered, but I couldn't stop her because I knew she needed to cry to let it all out before she could get better, so I just hugged her and held her throughout the time she let her tears out. I made circles on her back to soothe her from the torment of all that was happening in her mind. My tears were now relentless seeing her in this situation and I cried with her in that embrace trying to take that pain away from her. I would happily take that pain from her if it was possible. I wanted to take her far away from this place, from all the torturous memories and give her only happiness and peace.

She gradually improved, but her breathing remained high and shallow. Then, she apologized.

"Why?" I asked, "Why are you apologising?"

"For making you go through this with me. For insisting you to spend time with me so that I remember. You remembered everything and put yourself through seeing me for my sake. It must have been hard for you. I shouldn't have done that to you. It must have made it so much harder for you, me calling you. I understand now those longing and hurt in your eyes. I am so sorry."

I cupped her face with my palms, and reassured her, "Hey, it's not your fault, at all. Don't you dare be sorry for that? Don't you dare be sorry for anything? I agreed to help you, I agreed to stand by your side, and I stand by my word even today- more today. If anything, it was my fault and my cowardice. I am sorry so sorry. I didn't mean to hurt you like this. I didn't want you to go through all this."

She raised her eyes, finally looking at me but with guilt in her eyes or was it pity? I brought my face toward her, and our foreheads touched then I said, "Please don't feel sorry for me or sorry for putting me through this. If anything, I am glad you made that call. I am glad I get to see you and it made me realise-"

"Don't," she said slightly moving away and putting her hand on my lips. I gently removed her hands and entangling her hand with mine, I spoke, "I was stupid to jeopardise what we had. I am crazy about you T. I cannot go on like this forever without you. I cannot let you go. If anything, these past days have made me realise even more that I cannot let you go. I love you way too much for anything to stop me from feeling this way. All those months away from you were equally torture for me. I hated every waking moment. It was only when I heard your voice in the middle of the night, I felt relieved even if your voice did not recognise me."

She looked at me with all the love and hurt in her eyes and I feared that more tears were making its way through, but she shook her head and said, "I guess, I will keep on loving you, no matter what. But it's too late for us, isn't it?"

"I still love you the same, maybe even more. I am willing to fight for our love, more than I ever was. I am sorry for that night. I am sorry for letting you go and making both of us suffer."

I brought my hands to her shoulder, not being able to withstand her silence anymore I spoke, "Let's give us one more chance. We can remain friends if you can no longer trust me with your heart as long as you promise not to go around busting your head to forget me." I traced her scar on her head and my heart became heavy looking at her.

She wiped the tears from my cheek, I didn't even realise that my tears were still falling. She then spoke slowly, resting her hands on my cheek, "Aaron, think about it once. You don't want to disappoint your parents and I am not saying we should have a future together right now, but it will not do either of us any good. Do you think what we have is worth fighting for?"

"Yes, it is T. I am sorry it took us a toll to realise what we have. And these last few days have made me realise that I cannot let this go; not anymore. It is not too late, T. It is now late for us to back away from what we have."

"Tell me what is the purpose of it? We were separated a year ago."

When she said that it was as if air was sucked out of the room, and I was struggling to breathe. I looked at her with surprise and agony. Had she made up her mind to leave me? No, it cannot be happening. I could not possibly live without her. Not anymore. Not after all this.

For once, I really wanted to listen to my own voice and fight for my own choice.

"Lumanti, why did you decide to call me when you have forgotten all about me? Out of so many things you have forgotten, why did you want to relive this memory and find out more about a birthday reminder?"

She seemed to be lost in her thoughts by my questions, trying to find answers to what I had just asked. She hesitantly said, "I may have loved you in the past even in the moments when I forgot about your existence."

"T," I continued taking her out of her thoughts, "You wanted to talk to me, you wanted to seek me, this is a sign."

"Why? Why are you doing this?"

"Because I still love you. Even after all this time, I still do. I don't want to lose you again. I have understood it now. I will fight for what we have. I won't let us hurt again. I was blind not to see how I could have prevented it all from happening. I didn't even talk to them properly about us and gave up without even trying."

"What do you mean?" She asked looking puzzled.

"Do you love me?" I asked instead.

"Yes," she said without any hesitation.

"Even after all I have put you through?"

"It was not your fault."

"It was. My brain was not functioning that night. I was devastated that night. If my mom was not in the hospital, I would not have made that call."

"What? What had happened?" I could see from her expression that she looked troubled by this bit of information that I had withheld from her.

"She is fine now, much healthier. I didn't tell you because-because I don't know. I didn't want to worry you would be the right answer, right? But I don't know what I was thinking or what I was not thinking at that moment. I was so drained out that night. I broke too many things- your heart being the most important one." Maybe I did not tell her because I didn't want her to feel sorry for me and maybe I wanted to make it easy for her to hate me if I just broke it off. I cursed myself for not trying enough.

"T, do you trust me?"

"Of course I do." She whispered.

"I want to be with you. Please give me a chance." I added.

Chapter 23
Looking Forward

Lumanti

I didn't know what to say to him. Of course, I wanted to give us a second chance and make things right for once, but I was also scared of what it meant for us. What did the future hold for us? Why did he not tell me about his mother's condition? Will he tell me everything from now on?

He took a long breath and spoke, "I want you to trust me when I say this. I do not want to give up at all. I am just worried... I am scared that I would end up hurting you."

"Then don't...don't hurt me," that's all I could manage to say. I didn't want to be hopeful but hopeful I was- that he would make it right for us this time. Was I being an idiotic fool?

"Will you tell me everything from now on? Will you stop hiding things from me? No matter how cruel- no matter how serious?" I asked.

"I promise. I will. And I will tell you everything from now on and what happened in the past year when you were not around me. But I must warn you it is mostly sad." Then he paused and added, "And will you tell me if anything is bothering you or hurting you?"

"I will."

"And you can shout at me, scream at me if I am ever being an idiot." That earned a laugh from me and as I giggled, he brought his hands near my face, tucking a loose strand of hair behind my ears. Then, he just looked at me with warmth. *Would I be a fool if I called it love?*

While dragging his hand to my neck, he sighed before saying, "You must be tired, you haven't slept the whole night, so please try to sleep." Then he tried to stand to move away but I wrapped my hands around his wrist and whispered, "Stay."

He looked at me with pain in his eyes, then I pleaded, "Please just stay. Just lie down next to me."

He hesitated a little and slowly got into bed with me. He spooned me from behind and just like that we both drifted into a deep sleep- this time dream consisted of hope.

The sun was slowly making its way up and brightening the room. When I woke up, the other side of my bed felt cold in his absence. Had he left without even saying goodbye?

I suddenly heard some noise coming from the kitchen and as I followed the noise, I could see him moving around the kitchen. There was a pan already on the stove and several bowls were on the counter that he might be using to prepare food. It was therapeutic to see him go around the kitchen, fixing the meal, cleaning as he went, lost in his own world.

He was slightly startled when he caught me looking at him. "When did you wake up?"

"Just a moment ago." I shrugged and asked, "What are you cooking?"

"A little brekkie. I promise you; your kitchen is in good hands."

"I can see that," I said eyeing around the kitchen, which looked really clean unlike last time, when he was in the kitchen but of his place. The food was good, but the kitchen was a mess. I remembered telling him about the concept of cleaning as you go, which I could see him following through. I couldn't be any less proud. I chuckled.

"Let me help," I said moving towards kitchen, but he dragged me away and made me sit on the couch.

"You should be resting; I am almost done. I will plate the food and bring it to you."

"Bee, you don't have to," I said rising from my seat, but he gestured me not to and moved to the kitchen while saying, "I have to, and I want to."

He brought two cups of tea, smashed Avo toasties and omelet, then placed it on the coffee table with smile. I could not help but smile. We ate our breakfast in silence except when I told him everything tasted so good, and he thanked me for the compliment with his gorgeous smile. He even mentioned there is some left for Rianne. I almost forgot that she was here too.

He then pushed my plate a little nudging me to eat, "You need to finish them."

"I will," I sulked like a reprimanded kid.

Once we were done with breakfast I took our plates, though he insisted on taking them.

"You prepared breakfast, I should at least clear up the table," I said taking the plates to the kitchen. As I washed them, he cleaned the remainder of the kitchen. Out of nowhere, my mind started picturing what it would be like to live with this man and create a family of our own. And then I started imagining the little version of us running around in our little house. I shook my head and let that thought go. Could I dare to dream such a future with him? I realized after a while that he was looking at me curiously. Then he took my hand and gently pulled me towards him. We looked into each other's eyes, and it could be possible that briefly our eyes moved towards each other's lips, but we did not kiss. He touched my forehead with his and we stayed there for a moment. I wanted to hold onto this moment so badly. He slowly moved away and scooped me in his arms which earned him a little shriek from me, then he took me to my bedroom. He gently placed me on my bed and then he finally spoke,

"You need to rest. Don't go anywhere until I am back."

"Are you leaving already?" I asked rather disappointed that he was leaving so soon.

"I will be back soon. Last night I booked the flight for Adelaide, but it won't be long before I am back," he said reassuringly.

The mere few words shattered a recent dream that I had just conjured up in my mind. Would he be calling me like last time and breaking up with me? But there was nothing to break anymore so it should not matter what they say or what happens when he is there. Then I was hit with déjà vu that reminded me of our last conversation from last year right before he uttered heartbreaking words and with that realization, my heart started racing. I did not realize I was hyperventilating until I felt his hands on my arms and his words in my ears.

"T, hey look at me," he said searching my eyes and as my eyes darted towards him, he continued, "I will be back. I promise I will be back." But those were empty words for my brain and did nothing to soothe me because he had already broken that promise, just a year ago.

"Breathe T, here hold my hand and breathe with me. Breathe in. Breathe out. Breathe in.." he continued and slowly my heartbeat became normal. He sighed in relief and slumped to the ground as he put his head on my lap and continued with his chants of "I am sorry. I am so sorry."

A lone tear trickled through my eyes that dropped to his face joining the tears that were flowing from his eyes. I stroked his hair, and we stayed like that for a while. I slowly made him stand up and asked him to leave and reassured him with the same words I used last time, "I promise, I won't go anywhere."

He hugged me and planted a kiss on my forehead, then after a while he made his way out of my apartment. Unlike last time my heart was calmer and hopeful. Maybe I was no longer worried about him breaking my heart.

***

I lay down in my bed, a little more staring thoughtlessly at my ceiling. After a while, I stretched my arms and went to the bathroom to freshen up. When I came to the lounge dressed in my tank tops and sweatpants, I noticed Rianne was on the balcony.

"When did you wake up?" I asked as I walked towards her.

"Just a while ago. How are you doing? Is everything alright?" she asked, walking towards me rushing with concern.

"Yes, I am, in fact, I am much better. Thank you so much for everything." I said hugging her and she held onto me rubbing circles around my back. I was so grateful for her presence and for being there for me always throughout this time.

"I am glad you are doing fine," she said and looking around the apartment, she asked, "Where is Aaron?"

"Umm, he left earlier, said he had a flight," I replied making my way to the couch and added, "Oh, he had prepared some breakfast and left some for you too. It's in the fridge."

She smiled but instead of going to kitchen, she came and sat beside me, "Talk to me. What happened? What is going on?"

I couldn't help it, so I told Rianne about my recent conversation with Aaron, what happened in the past from my recovered memories and why he had left just now to go catch that flight. I also expressed my concern if I should be hopeful at this. After I finished telling her everything, she pulled me into a hug and told me that everything would be alright and that she was glad that my memory was back.

I was glad too. It was not fun not knowing certain parts of your life, no matter how hurtful they were. Many things around my mind started to make sense now.

After a moment, she added, "Focus on yourself first, Hun. It is time for Aaron to take some action and decide about where he wants to take it and while he makes that decision, you cannot forsake your own priorities in the process."

"I guess you are right," I agreed.

Then, I realized while I was pouring out my troubles to her, I forgot to ask about what was going on in her life. I remembered that she had a date, so I asked her, "Enough about me, tell me about your date last night."

She blushed when I mentioned it. I had never seen her blush in my entire life.

"It was great. It was like a picnic under the stars. We talked and talked for so long. We got along so well and there were no awkward conversations ever between us. I was so glad we could do that. With her even the silence was comfortable." She was smiling widely now, and I couldn't help but be happy for my best friend.

"Aww, that sounds so cute. I am glad it went great," I mentioned and then asked rather sneakily, "And did you kiss her?"

"Oh my god! Ray, at one point, I just wanted to kiss her, but I didn't. I didn't know if it was right timing yet."

That statement shocked me, so I had to ask, "Since when did you start thinking about timing?"

"I know right. Since her I guess," she said while smiling sheepishly.

I could feel that she was serious about her, and I was glad that Sara could be that person for her. Sara was an amazing person with such a pure soul and kind heart. Both of them would make a great pair and I told her the same.

"Even yesterday, when I found you like that," she shuddered a little and a rush of guilt came over me, while she continued, "Sara was so helpful. She told me how to talk to you and she was there guiding me through the process. Oh, I forgot to tell you, she is coming here to see you if that is alright with you."

"It's totally fine. I have to thank her as well." I spoke.

"She is probably on the way."

"So, you are really serious about her, huh?"

"Kind of yeah. I really want to ask her to be my girlfriend, but I am not sure, if she is ready yet?"

"Why don't you ask her?" I suggested when I saw a shadow pass at the door.

"Do you think she will be ok with it?" Rianne asked.

"Well, you can ask her now, she is standing right behind you," I stated while smiling and looking at Sara who was now inside the room. The color of Rianne's face disappeared, and she abruptly turned behind to face Sara.

"I am sorry, I didn't mean to eavesdrop, but the door was open, so I walked in when I heard your voice," Sara began and then paused before asking while looking at the ground, "Umm so you were trying to ask me something?"

Rianne stood up from where she was sitting and walked towards her, "I would love to do it in a grand fashion but as you may have already heard, I really would like to call you my girlfriend if you would you like. Would you like to be my girlfriend?"

She smiled widely and said, "Yes, I would love to." Then, Rianne pulled her into a kiss, and I discreetly tried to walk away to the balcony to give them privacy. But before I could do that, they moved away. Sara then spoke to me, "So silly of me, how are you doing now, Lumanti?"

"Call me Ray. Thank you so much for yesterday. I am doing much better now."

"I am glad you are." She said rubbing my shoulder.

"I am so happy for you two," I exclaimed and hugged them both.

Later, Rianne mentioned that she had already ordered some Thai food and it was on the way. Meanwhile, I plated them the food Aaron had prepared in the morning.

Later in the evening, Rianne and Sara left. Once, I was left to my own devices, I lay down, thinking and processing last night and everything after it- all over again.

Chapter 24
An Overdue Conversation

Aaron

"Mom?"

"Outside, in the backyard," she responded.

She was tending her small garden. She planted more flowers this time than last year. There were different shades of flower and a few green herbs.

"It is so hard to maintain them at this time of year. We must be extra careful and tend them well especially at the beginning so that they will grow properly and adapt well with the circumstances," she said tending a plant in front of her when I joined her.

It felt like it was directed more at me than lessons on plants, but I did not say anything. I had been out of touch with everyone lately because I was not in the right state of mind for the past year. I was angry most of the time and avoided conversations as much as possible. Ever since my mother came home from hospital, our conversations were mostly about her health, and I avoided talking about the night when dad and Meekha showed up after admitting mom in hospital only to find me distraught for whole another reason. Mom tried to bring it up once, but I simply mentioned that I didn't want to talk about it. When she tried to talk about it regardless, I cut the call. I visited occasionally during the festival or functions and kept myself to my previous room or helping around but kept my words to minimum. Maybe that's why when I showed up late last night, they didn't say anything and just exchanged looks among each other.

"Do you have anything to tell me?" she asked when I just stared at the flowers, she had planted without saying anything.

"Well, yes, but how did you know?" I inquired.

"Because I am your mother," she said in a matter-of-fact tone. All night I have been trying to form well put sentences and arguments to tell her all about it. I had never got a chance to tell her before this about Lumanti. As I tried to recall the lines I had practiced, all I could blurt out was, "It is about Lumanti. I love her." That was not what I had planned to say at all, but my mouth decided not to listen to my mind.

"You do?" She looked at me suspiciously.

"Mom, she is really a great girl. You would love her. You need to give her a chance."

"*Chhora*, I never said I wouldn't give her a chance. It is you who never gave her a chance and your relationship a chance in front of us. Yes, we wanted you to marry someone with the same background and culture as ours but not at the cost of losing you."

"I thought you wouldn't agree."

"Maybe we would or maybe we wouldn't have but you never asked."

"Now I am asking," I said while plucking weeds from the ground.

"What exactly are you asking? To marry her? I think it was your words that you are too young to get married." I had told my parents to stop the marriage proposal with the same excuse.

"Yes, I am but when I can, I would like to spend my life with her, only her. I don't want to lose her again."

"Again?"

I then told her everything- what had happened last year, our history and our recent conversation. As I shared all of this, I came to realise that I had never talked with my mother this much for this long. She smiled, frowned, nodded, reacting to me but never once did she interrupt me. She just listened.

"I just did not want to disappoint you and dad, so I never really tried but I am willing to now because I think I will be forever angry and disgruntled if I don't," I said looking at the ground.

My mother finally spoke after hearing everything I had to say, "I hear you and I understand, where you are coming from but was it really you not wanting to disappoint us or was it you not being sure if this relationship will grow?"

"Mom, I am sure of this," I defended.

She gently ran her hand through my hair while saying, "You are all grown up now. It is your life. We are not here to judge you; we are just going to guide you. The rest is up to you. You need to know if it's worth it otherwise it is better to endure a little bit of sorrow now to avoid a lifetime of pain. Don't be stubborn or rebellious about it."

"That night I was not in the right space of mind."

"Your dad wouldn't have been so angry and harsh about it if he had not seen you like the way he saw you that day. He cares for you. You need to realize if it is worth fighting for when you have tried to avoid this battle for so long. I am not going to tell you to stop seeing her, it's up to you. You don't have to get married now. I also want you to be capable enough before you get married, but I want you to know the person you are marrying properly before you get into it. Think with a clear head and we will support it no matter what it is as long as it makes you happy. She seems like a lovely girl, but you shouldn't ruin her life in your stubbornness to get what you want. You are old enough now; you need to think about the consequences and the future."

***

Deep down in my heart, I knew that my mother was right. Deep in my heart I also knew that Lumanti was the one. As I tried to listen to my own voice amidst all the noise, her face appeared in front me.

A beautiful memory perched in my mind of the time when she and I laid on the bare ground, looking at the blue sky, watching clouds pass by. She was giggling at something that I had told her- it was a beautiful sound. She was looking at the sky but all I could do was look at her and listen to her melodic laughter. I knew then like I knew now that I could never get tired of listening to her laughter.

She was always so sure of herself, doing what she pleased and finding happiness in little pieces. When I was at my lowest, she would come around and just stay by my side sometimes with silence sometimes with wisdom of her words. It was ecstatic in that little bubble we lived in, until the day it popped.

When I reached my room after talking to my mother, lost in thought, I noticed that I had left the room earlier in a mess. There was an unmade bed, clothes coming out of the open suitcase, a desk full of clutter. My room's state was what my mind felt like. I picked up my clothes from the floor and went to sit in bed.

I was once again filled with the same questions and thoughts of Lumanti in my head. *How did I not fight enough for this? Why did I let other people dictate my feelings? I am a fool to realize it now. Am I even worthy of someone like her? Will I ruin her if I got too close to her?*

I didn't even realize that my father had come to my room until he spoke, "You know it was your mother's decision for us to come here. I didn't want to come here at all at first, but she insisted that for the future of you and your sister we needed to leave."

I was startled by his presence. We hadn't had a proper conversation between us since that night, except for occasional light talk when I was on call with mom to ask her about her health. So, I was naturally surprised when he talked to me in all seriousness but there was no hint of sternness like he used to have. He sat beside me on the bed and continued, "She prepared everything. I was too angry to help her with anything. I am glad of her decision now. I am glad of the life we got to give you and your sister. Having said that, I was and am always scared of what the culture here would do to our traditions. So, I tried to keep it close, to make sure that we didn't forget our roots."

I assumed mom had told him already about what I had told her earlier. I didn't know what to say to what he had just told me, but I really needed to tell him this,

"Dad... I... I no longer know what I should be doing. I really tried to do what you wanted me to do. I had convinced myself that I should leave her and follow through my parents' decision but dad, I love her so much and I don't want to keep on losing her repeatedly and again in my life. I am sorry for misbehaving last time but it was not because of her but rather the thought of losing her. Will you please give us a chance? At least meet her once. If you still don't like her, then I will never bring this up." I brought my both hands to my face and moved it across my head in frustration. Then he brought his hand over my shoulder and patted on it.

Next, he said, "My entire life, my parents made my decisions for me- big or small, so naturally I thought I should make your decisions too. I had never wanted anything or anyone as passionately as you do so maybe I failed to understand where you were coming from. It was not fair to you."

He looked up at the ceiling lost in his thoughts for a moment. "Although my parents did find me your amazing mother who gave me these amazing kids to call mine- so no regrets there," he smiled looking at me and I could see his eyes glistening which made me welled up a little.

And, he continued, "But I am not sure if I will be able to find an amazing wife for you. You will be the one who will spend the rest of your life with your partner, not us. If you think she is the one, then you should go for it. It is time you do what you want to do and not what I want for you. For me, your happiness is of utmost importance."

"Thank you so much dad." Overwhelmed by what my father had just told me, I hugged him and without any of us noticing, we might have shed a few tears at that moment.

I couldn't believe how I let my own mind stop from following my heart. If only I had, try to talk to them properly about us and not gave up without even trying.

Chapter 25
Loving You

Lumanti was sitting on a small stool by the balcony looking outside and soaking in the sun. The weather was beautiful. The sky was clear and mostly blue with white cotton like clouds moving around. She had a book in her hand that she had planned to read but instead of delving into the words of the book, she was lost, somewhere far beyond. She was thinking about Aaron and the time they kissed- the night before their breakup. They had never kissed so passionately as if their life depended on it. She was in love with the guy she could not have. She had always understood his respect for his parents, and she had always admired that about him so she could not let herself be the reason for him going against his family. In mixture of fear of losing him and love for him, she could not help but kiss him one last time before they parted again. She wanted to keepsake that memory for lifetime while she prepared herself for the worst. To regain that memory was like regaining a precious treasure for her even though that memory hurts her, it was something incredibly significant.

Aaron's parents were no longer objecting, perhaps they never would have if he had been a good communicator. She on the other hand had to try convincing her own parents about it. Her mom was understanding but her dad was relentless. Though she could see the wall chipping off slowly.

After all the miscommunications, it was up to these two star-struck lovers to decide the fate of their relationship.

She had recently downloaded all the photos from her camera onto her tablet. As she sat by the balcony sliding through the memory lane of past years and a year before that, she heard a knock at her front door, surprised by the knock, she hurriedly went towards the door. Outside the door was Aaron in a white shirt, black jeans and a flower bouquet in his hand smiling at her. She smiled back and took the bouquet from him. He then swooped her into his arms and kissed her like he was kissing her for the first time.

"I love you. I love you so much."

"I love you more. I take it the conversation went well," she said cupping his face.

"Well, I am no best friend with my mom... or dad, like you are with yours but somehow, I felt I could tell her anything and she would have listened to me, and I realized how I never tried enough to talk with her. This time, I told her everything T, and all she ever wanted was to hear my side of story. And she told me to be sure of this relationship and not to jeopardise your life in process of figuring this out."

He then proceeded to tell her about his recent conversation with both his parents.

"I guess, miscommunication played a better role than us in this relationship," she said with a ghost of a smile.

"Yeah, or lack of communication from my side," he added and continued, "I can't do this back and forth. Let's get done with this already. Tell me what do you want out of this relationship? Do you trust me? Do you think we can work this out?"

"I would love to think that we can. Don't you think we can?"

"I would keep on loving you even if you asked me not to. I am sorry for hurting you and making you upset. I will make it up to you. Can we please give this love a second chance?"

"Do you promise not to break my heart?"

"I could never." Both of their eyes were glistening as they expressed their love for each other.

"Seal it with a kiss then," she said smirking at him. Without wasting any second, he pulled her towards him by the waist and dipping forward, he initiated the kiss. As their arms entwined with each other, their tongues danced in the known rhythm. Soon their hands were all over each other's body, as if they had been deprived of each other's touch for so long.

The day and the night passed in each other's embrace. The next morning during breakfast, Aaron told Lumanti while sitting with their fingers entangled, in a patio chair that she had set up in the balcony, but the question loomed in their heads, "What next?"

"How do we go from here?" Both spoke at the same time and chuckled at how they were both thinking about the same thing.

Aaron gestured her with his hand to go ahead and she said, "I think we should take it slow. I don't want us to rush into anything."

Aaron nodded in understanding and agreed with her, "Sure, if it would make you happy and keep your mind at ease."

After a moment, he added, "So no marriage proposal, huh?" Lumanti was surprised to hear him say that, but she soon noticed the fake pout followed by a smile lurking on his face letting her know that he was joking. She gently pushed him away and they started laughing. He then pulled her towards him and kissed her forehead.

While they were sitting restfully in each other's presence with comfortable silence, Lumanti's phone started ringing and she went inside to take the call. When she came out of the room, she was jumping in excitement.

"Who was it? What happened?" Aaron asked walking in.

"You know the job I applied at the studio?" she started.

She didn't have to say anything, he could read from her expression that she had got her dream job. So, he simply said with a wide smile, "You got it didn't you?" She nodded, tapping her feet in excitement. "Wow, that's amazing. Congratulations," Aaron added with smile and hugged her but somehow his excitement did not meet his eyes.

Lumanti had landed her dream job, but she would now have to move within a month to a new city in another state and Aaron was aware of it. Though he was happy for Lumanti, a selfish part of his heart wanted to spend a little more time with her before they had to deal with the complication of distance.

"Will you have to move soon?" he asked cautiously.

Slowly moving her face away but still staying within his embrace, she said looking at him, "Umm, I might have to start the role by the next month. So, I will probably have to go by the end of this month to settle down and find a place to stay."

"Oh Okay," He responded with tight lipped smile.

"It might give us some time to work out things between us." Lumanti said reassuringly.

"But what is there left to work out?" He replied defensively.

"Well, a lot. So much has happened within the last year and these past few weeks."

"And you think this distance between us will help?" he asked skeptically.

"It will be hard, but it might help us see things in clearer perspective."

"T, I am happy for you. I really am. But if I am being honest, I don't want to be away from you anymore. A year away was enough for me."

"I understand. But this time we will be talking with each other despite the distance."

"You will be by yourself. There is no one you know. Maybe I should come there too."

"What? And leave your work behind?" Lumanti said, surprisingly.

"I will be fine. I will manage. I can get a similar role there."

"B, I am just going to another state. Not entirely different country. I can come back here anytime I want. And I think if we can work this out, we will be able to make things a bit better for both of us. Should I not go?"

"No, no. I didn't mean that. I know how much it means to you. We will figure it out. I just wish it was not this soon. Let me come with you."

Putting her palm in his chest, she said, "B, listen, I understand that lot is happening here between us, and this distance might complicate things, but we will get through this, and you have recently landed a job that you have been working so hard for. I don't want you to leave that behind for me."

"B are you okay?" she asked with her voice full of concern when he didn't respond to anything and just looked at the ground.

"Yes, I am fine," He looked up from the ground and to her face, "Will you be fine? And you had better be careful walking around the city and especially the stairs. You will be extra careful, won't you? Please tell me you will."

As soon as what Aaron had said dawned on her, she brought her fingers to his lips to calm his stress-talking and moved forward to nestle into his chest.

***

It has been six months since the last time they won over their love, all over again. And it had been three months since Lumanti was back in Sydney and working remotely with the same studio. Eventually, she convinced her employer that she could work independently and remotely from another state as she couldn't get used to being in the new city all by herself. But most importantly she was missing her home, which she had started to find in a particular person. Lumanti and Aaron were now living together in Aaron's place- which was technically his parents' place that he was renting.

"As much as I want to sit right by your side, next to you, we have to leave. Remember, the errand that my dad had asked for. Would you still like to come with?" Aaron said to Lumanti who had her head on his chest cuddling him on the couch.

"Yes, of course, what was it again?" she asked drawing circles on his chest while his hand lightly rubbed against her shoulder.

"It is a function that he couldn't attend so he wants me to go. It is sort of a formal event. Sorry, to drag you to this one."

"No problem at all love, sure let's go," she said getting up from the couch but then he pulled her in for one more kiss before letting her go.

After half an hour, Aaron came out of the room looking poised in his black and white suit while Lumanti looked drop dead gorgeous in her sleeveless long black dress. She was wearing a dangling silver earring, and her hair was updo. Aaron could not take his eyes off her. He was spellbound, all over again.

He approached towards her and giving her his arms, he said, "Shall we?"

She smiled gently and said, "We shall."

"The event is at Uni?" she asked when Aaron parked his car in one of the parking lots of the Uni.

"Umm yes, it is an event in relation to International students," he fumbled, "He has funded this event, so I just have to go and show the presence."

There was a welcome sign board on the entrance of the venue. They walked towards the venue and greeted people around. Aaron seemed too distracted or rather bored.

"I am bored," Aaron said and added, "Let's explore the Uni at night."

"What are you talking about? Don't you think we need to stay a little longer? The event has just started."

"Ah, they will survive," He said checking his phone and added, "Let's go."

As they walked through the path, her hand in his arms, they were reminded of their first encounter and many other encounters that led their path to them. Then suddenly Aaron moved forward towards a building by himself, saying something and disappeared inside.

"B, wait." Lumanti said, following him- not able to meet his pace in those high heels.

The place was dark, and she could not see him or anything at all.

"B, are you here? Are you okay? Love?"

Then a static noise could be heard in the dark followed by an echo of thump.

Love was merely just another word to me until you came along.

A voice came out of the darkness.

A smile spread across her face as soon as she recognized the voice. The voice continued.

I was simply lost until I found you.

It's a miracle, truly to have you in my life

To lose you to the fate

And have you back in my life

I got to thank my lucky stars

And I have got to tell you how much in love I am with you.

I wouldn't be lying when I say I want to spend the rest of my life with you and more.

As if on cue the light fell on the room and the whole room was bright, filled with all her loved ones, both their families. The string of lights was arranged by the window. The wine glasses and champagne flutes were ready to be filled.

And Aaron was on one knee in front of her.

"Lumanti Ray Jones, would you like to spend the rest of your years with me? Will you marry me?"

Lumanti was shocked and the words were lost in her when she saw what he had done and how much effort he had put into making this all happen. He managed to convince all hers and his family members to be in this same room. All of them were looking expectantly at her for an answer when she realized that she had not given her answer yet.

"Oh my god. Yes, a hundred times yes." she said as she went on her knee with him and faced him.

Everybody cheered for them, and they hugged each other tightly as they decided to hold on to each other for their lifetime.

Chapter 26
The Next Step

Aaron

My hands were sweating, and I was nervous the entire time leading to the proposal. It was going to be the last thing that I hid from her. I had contacted her parents, apologised, and promised to take care of their daughter and forever cherish her. Both her parents were happy and forgiving. I was glad they agreed for my proposal to ask for their daughter's hand in marriage. Her father with not much of subtlety warned me of the consequences if I were ever to hurt his daughter. I would not never dream of it even if there was no threat of him maiming me.

My voice was shaky and ever so nervous when I did that declaration of love for her in the room full of our loved ones. When the light fell on her face, I saw her smiling with her eyes glistening ever so slightly but when she didn't answer for a moment, my heart started beating faster and faster. Upon realising her lack of words over my proposal, she quickly chanted her range of yeses then I relaxed a little.

Since that day my heart had been singing only the happy songs; I was whistling and daydreaming. We decided to remain engaged and get married only a year after because there was a lot to prepare for and a career to manage. We also needed to find our footing back in our relationship. Secure those lost and found memories.

Lumanti and I spent most of our time together, rekindled the old spark, planned ideas for a wedding, fought a little over it. During these times, our parents caught up to discuss further on the wedding and it was an amazing feeling to see them sitting with us, discussing about the wedding plans and preparation. After a lengthy discussion, we came to terms that we would be having two kinds of wedding, one in Australia to appease her dad's side of the family and the wedding fulfilling all Newar customs to appease her mom's and my side of the family. My family wanted to do it in Nepal for the latter one because most of the family especially my grandparents were in Nepal, and we agreed without any hesitation.

Regardless, I was excited to marry the love of my life any number of times it required. The more time I spent with her, the more I realized that it would be blissful to spend the rest of my life with her.

Just like that getting lost in her lovely eyes, the time flew by and the day leading to the series of events and functions for our wedding arrived.

For the first part of our wedding, we, along with our family agreed to organize it at the beach in front of T's uncle's (her dad's brother's) beach house. We wanted to keep this part of the wedding chic and minimalistic. The event planners turned the dock area of the house into a beautiful set-up with flowers, drapes, and lights. All our family and few of our close friends were in attendance. Adam and Liam were also present. Adam brought his fiancé as his date while Liam arrived without one. Rianne stood happily beside her date Sara, who I finally got to be properly introduced after Lumanti and I made up. Samantha, T's friend from Uni was also there but she also, like Liam did not have any date. From corner of my eye, I noticed some flirtations being passed around them, but I couldn't investigate further into it as didgeridoo started playing and my beautiful bride made her way towards me.

She was adorned in a red ombre off-the-shoulder mermaid gown while she walked down the aisle with both her parents beside her. She was breathtaking and I couldn't tear my eyes away from her. It stayed locked in hers as her eyes locked in mine. I could not believe that we were getting married. She was going to be my wife. I quickly wiped the lone tear that had escaped from eyes. After the ceremony, her dad gave us two stones to cast into the sea. He added when handing us those stones, "It is to signify for you to stay together as life flows ups and downs."

Lumanti went to hug him, and both shed a little tear. He patted my back and after wiping his tears, he gestured to me and T, to cast away the stones. And we did the same.

The reception was booked in a lovely venue with a high ceiling and a beautiful chandelier. The only two things my bride wanted. During the reception, there were a few special toasts followed by the funny ones and there also was a threatening one from Rianne about how I must not hurt Lumanti, or else? I wouldn't dare to.

Lumanti danced with both her parents and then she and I showcased the miserably choreographed dance that we had learned from YouTube, but everybody said it was beautiful. So, it must have been but Lumanti, did not believe it. Later everyone joined the dance floor with their partners.

All of us danced the night away and there were some fireworks in the background as the night set in. It was a night to remember.

***

I had already seen her as my bride mere weeks ago but seeing her again adorned in bridal red and gold Brocade saree and shawl along with Newar jewellery, my heart skipped a beat. All I could do was look at her in awe and full of love. If anybody was talking to me now, I was quite sure that I didn't hear them because my wife's beauty was taking all the attention that I had to give. We carried out one ritual after ritual, putting vermillion on her forehead, then exchanging garland and our rings. As we move close to the end of the first set of ritual, Lumanti was advised to bow down to my feet which caught both of us by surprise. When her mother was going to guide her to do it, I stopped them, asking not to. However, all the relatives insisted that she must, and she simply gave me a look to suggest that it was ok, and she was going to do it. I was not sure if she was comfortable with it but surely, I was not. Once she got up, I couldn't resist so I bowed myself to her feet because if she were to revere me as a god, then I must do the same because she was my goddess.

This led for some of the relative to leave snarky comments, "She has already got him wrapped around his finger." One needn't understand the language when their expressions were too loud and I would have given them my piece of mind but while they were leaving the snarky comments, our younger cousins cheered their approval in our support in loud noise, which I really appreciated. She looked at me with pure admiration and love. After that she was taken away to complete the remaining rituals for which I was not supposed to be present.

As I moved towards to put on my shoes, I realised that it was gone. Meekha and my cousins did nothing to protect it then. They must have nicked it during the middle of the ceremony because I was fairly sure, Meekha took my shoes the moment I took it off. As I recall Meekha's wedding I was not even present in this part of the ceremony because our cousin sisters had already hidden the shoes and the negotiation between bride and groom's side had already started.

All the young ones from her side of the family must have worked up a really good plan to hide my shoes as a part of the custom, even though my side tried their best to jeopardize that plan of theirs. There were elderly family members who did not approve of the customs, but they did it anyway. I personally did not mind and was prepared to give them money as well. I felt that it was a fun icebreaker for the two sides of the family to come together and enjoy the function while the long marriage ceremony continued. Both parties negotiated rather heavily upon the price of my hostage shoes. I was enjoying the whole debacle. As they settled down, I gave them a whole wad of money and they gave me my shoes. It turned out to be rather expensive shoes but anything to see those happy winning faces.

A hearty meal was put in front of me to eat but all I could think was about her. I had just seen her, and they took her away so soon. I knew it was only for another ritual and part of the process, but I was missing her already. I was not going to let her be out of my sight once we got to our home. I did not even have any appetite to eat when she was running in my mind. And I kept on wondering if she ate at all. I knew how tolling these events were.

When I finally got to see her, she was crying, and concern clutched in my chest. "What's wrong? Why is she crying?" I asked my sister, taking one step to walk towards Lumanti.

Meekha held me by my arms to stop and explained wiping her own tears, "She is saying goodbye to her family and with so much happening, it is a natural reaction." It must have been overwhelming for her with all the attention and those lengthy rituals; she must have been going through upheaval of emotions to make her cry like that. My tears were making their way to my eyes when she started crying on her mother's shoulders. I wanted to scoop her in my arms and make her feel better. Soon, I will do that. I quickly wiped out the lone tear daring to escape and waited for them to let me take my bride with me.

Her mother's brother carried her on his back and circled the car that we would be going home to as per the ritual. Then they put a red shawl on top of the car for auspiciousness, and then sent us away with heavy hearts and good wishes.

When we reached our house, my mother welcomed us. She let Lumanti hold one end of the keys that she was holding and asked her to follow her.

When we reached the lounge area where another set of ritual were to happen, it was my younger cousins' turn to block her way and for this part, she would have to bribe them with money to pass. I secretly handed her a wad of money to give it to them assuming she would not know about this part of the custom but to my surprise, she flashed a smile, taking the money I had given and adding more to that stack of money, she handed it to them which led them to part the way for their new sister-in-law. She giggled in response. It was good to hear that sound after seeing her cry most of the car ride. This must have helped her take mind off all the emotions.

There were more rituals again after that day. We had to visit different temples. I had to go to her side of the family to be introduced to each member of the family she had. After everything was done and dusted, we travelled to more parts of Nepal and went on our own adventure that we had promised to each other. I was excited to go on this whole new adventure of life with her. I would go anywhere she would take me.

Chapter 27
Memories to Keepsake

Lumanti

I woke up in his arms, like I did last morning and a morning before and every morning since we had been blissfully married to each other. And every morning I felt grateful to wake up next to his calm, relaxed face and cherished the mornings I would wake up with him peppering kisses all over my face and body. It had been two months since we got back home from our elaborate wedding and extended honeymoon and though the time had passed, the memories of our past few months were still fresh like it was yesterday.

I was in a sheer shock when I saw the room full of our loved ones and when he went down on his knees, I couldn't help but feel nervous and excited at the same time. I almost forgot to give an answer as I was spellbound by the whole arrangement. I went on my knees with him after telling him yes, a couple of times and more. A year later we celebrated the first wedding ceremony in Australia by the beach. With all our loved ones, cheering for us, dancing with us, it was a beautiful wedding.

A week from beach wedding, we rushed to Nepal for the wedding to be conducted as per Newar customs with both our families. If I had thought it was hectic with two events and bachelorette planning in Australia, Nepal was on another level, the whole process was so surreal and frenzied at the same time. If it had not been for the big family in Nepal and all the families joining from all over the world, helping me with the preparation, I would have gone crazy. I was sad that Rianne could not make it to this part of wedding though she really wanted to, so I kept on sending her pictures every time I got a chance to. My cousins were amazing and immensely helpful. In fact, thanks to them, I did not have to do anything except to sit patiently for most of the time. Everything had been taken care of and for once I was not bothered to worry about how I wanted things to be. I just let it be. During all these preparations time, Aaron and I had not got any time to spend together properly. We always had to sneak out of our own functions to meet each other and spend some quality time. I was beginning to miss him so much. When I found out that in some of the functions, that he would not be there with me or more so that he should not be there, made me miss him even more and wanted to get done with all these functions as soon as possible.

That's why when he showed up uninvited in our girls' night, I was so happy for his intrusion while the girls not so much.

Before the main functions started my cousins in Nepal, prepared a girls' night at a resort where they had a booked a cabin for the night. They called the night Kwo: Ceremony for we would be putting on Kwo: a kind of natural scrub that would make our skin healthy and make it glow. It was the ground mixture of flowers, maize and other ingredients which had to be mixed with mustard oil and scrubbed into the face and body. Riya, one of my cousins, mentioned to me, "It used to be a typical part of the wedding, a very long time ago and it had stopped. People do other functions inspired by Indian customs these days, but we wanted to organize this function for you." I was grateful for their gesture, and it was such a relaxing thing to do as well. We drank, danced, and made a whole event out of it. It was so sweet of them to include Meekha as well.

I could not spend much time with Meekha, Aaron's sister during our first wedding function but in Nepal, she took me to so many different places and shared with me her experiences at the Newar wedding. She was happily married and staying in Nepal with her husband, but they usually do back and forth in between Nepal and Australia. I found out that she got married during our breakup, otherwise, maybe I would have attended the wedding too. I asked her curiously, "Did Aaron bring any dates during your wedding?"

To which Meekha laughed, "No, he was mostly running around like a sad puppy throughout my wedding. It was sad to see him then but now that I see how happy he is with you, that memory just feels funny to me as a sister." I laughed with her, and I noticed how big and beautiful her eyes were, maybe that's why they named her Meekha, eyes in Newar language. His entire family seemed to have good genetics in a beauty standard.

She then added, "Speaking of my brother, let me send him a picture of his bride."

I posed for the picture making funny face. After a few moments, he called Meekha and asked to speak with me. "Hey *mero mutu*," he spoke, and I blushed immediately upon his choice of words. He had been calling me that ever since we started living together from our engagement. As he was on speaker, everybody heard him calling me *his heart* and teased me with their set of "aww" "ooo..." I couldn't help but blush even more. We had to cut our call shortly after.

All the girls were dancing and drinking, when suddenly we heard a knock at the door of the cabin we were staying in. It was Aaron, I couldn't help but hug him upon seeing him and then asked, "What are you doing here?"

"I was missing you and I had to see you. You look so gorgeous."

"I look like a mess, but I am glad you are here. I missed you too." I hugged him and then he pulled me in for a kiss. I couldn't wait for us to finish these functions and go to our home, sleeping and waking up in his arms every day, every night, every waking moment.

After a couple of days, the Lakha: ceremony arrived, the next important event in which his side of the family would bring lots of gifts including jewellery, and beauty products to present to me. In this function, as well, Aaron did not get to come but only his family would be visiting me for the traditional pre-wedding rituals which served as an agreement between the families for this marriage.

My mother's side of the grandparents wanted to organize a mini reception with the family in Nepal as they couldn't be part of the reception in Sydney. They insisted that it had to be separate from the reception that the groom would throw. There had to be two different receptions from the bride's side for her side of the family before the main wedding day and there would be another thrown by the groom's side for his side of the family after the wedding day. The bride would be present on the groom's side of the reception however, the groom would not usually be present on the bride's side of the reception. When my grandparents said small reception, I assumed it was for close people and the number would be less than fifty but that turned out to be a joke, there were 500 people invited and according to my grandfather, he was not happy that he had to cut out some names from the list. I was shocked and more surprised when my mom told me that her parents wanted to spend money on this reception. They couldn't do the same for my mom because she married my dad when she was in Australia and my grandparents visited for their ceremony rather than being able to organize anything from their end, so my mom did not stop them from doing what they want to do for my wedding. It was a heartfelt gesture, and I was grateful for their presence in my life.

When I told Aaron about the number of guests, he told me that it was normal. His side of the party was going to have a similar number of people too. No wonder they have separate reception from each side, I thought.

It was a surprise that I hadn't fainted out of the sheer excitement and overwhelmingness of the number of functions we were going through in these past weeks. Soon enough the wedding day, also known as Swoyambar, arrived and it was the most hectic day of all. I was adorned in a beautiful red and gold brocade saree with intricate design laced all around it. They put on all sorts of gold jewellery on me and wearing all of that was already tiring for me. Everyone was running around making sure things were going well. My dad and family from down under were mostly confused, but they did their best to help around and get things done. Everyone was wearing different hues of red and pink looking gorgeous in their attire. My mom on the other hand, looking equally breathtaking in red, seemed happy yet emotional all the time. Tears were always on the verge of spilling. My father seemed more emotional these days too, probably all the functions and celebrations and the energy of it taking a toll on his well hid emotions. Being back with her family and knowing most of the rituals, my mom guided me through it all patiently while explaining different meanings behind them. I was in awe of knowing all those meaning that each ritual and process held.

Riya, was putting on a red paint-like liquid, called *Ala:* around my feet when my mom walked in the room.

"*Tataa*," an endearing term that Riya called me to address me as I was older than her, "it is all done, and you are looking so pretty."

I thanked her and then she ran outside as she remembered something that her mom told her to do.

My mom walked towards me and gently put her hand on my head and kissed my forehead. She wiped a slight tear from the corner of her eyes before it could fall. I leaned my head against her body and just stayed there hugging her from where I was seated, like a little girl.

"Janti is here" someone shouted from somewhere and everyone rushed out. Janti would be a procession of the groom's side of the family along with music and a live band of *Newa: baja:* (instruments). I could hear from a distance the sound of the flute at first followed by a mixture of different instruments coming together making a beautiful melody. Aaron had told me that though being a Newar, Baja were used by only certain Newar community, but he still pulled it off because he preferred it over the loud bands of music.

As I walked towards where he was sitting in front of our families and the priest, I could not take my eyes off him. He looked so handsome in his suit with the essence of Newar fabric surrounding the edges and a *bhadgaule topi*, which was like a cap, but it was more upward facing and black in colour. I had seen him as a groom already but the warm feeling around my chest was still the same upon seeing him. Then the love I had for him hit me, I was utterly and truly in love with this man. When I looked at him, he felt like a home to be, my safe place, someone who brought calmness to my racing heart.

The entire wedding event was one of the most memorable moments of my life. It was not only a celebration of love, but it also brought me closer to my roots and taught me a lot about marriage and my love for my partner. After the wedding ceremony, we had a wonderful honeymoon where we spent most of it, exploring Nepal's glorious nature and enjoying each other's company. It was a time for us to unwind and cherish the beautiful moments that life had bestowed upon us.

During this wedding period and once we were back, I got to know more about Aaron's family, including his parents and sister. They welcomed me with open arms and showed me a lot of kindness. His father, who initially seemed quite strict and stern, turned out to be a wonderful and enjoyable person to be around. He had a great sense of humour and loved sharing stories about his life. His mother, on the other hand, was the epitome of kindness and warmth. She had a heart of gold and always made sure that Aaron took good care of me. Sometimes I wish I had met them earlier; however, I was grateful to be a part of this wonderful family at present and it made my heart swell with happiness. It was a heartwarming experience to see how much they cared for my husband, and how they welcomed me into their family with so much love.

After travelling around in Nepal as part of our honeymoon, we came back to our cozy home. We were no longer renting his parents' place because his father gave it to us as our wedding gift. I was taken aback by his gesture.

I was grateful for it and felt blessed for the chance that I would be able to raise my kids in the same house where my husband was raised. My husband- it was the most beautiful feeling to be able to call him my husband now. Someone I loved, lost, and found again. I was never letting him go now.

***

"T, our post-wedding and wedding photos have arrived, do you want to see them?" Aaron called from the study.

"Oh my god, is it here already?" I said excitedly.

"Yep, do you want to see?"

I ran to the study where he was. He was sitting in a swivel chair in front of the computer on his desk with his glasses. He looked so sexy with his glasses on. I went to sit on his lap and saw the e-mail he was looking at. Holding me by my waist and kissing me on the neck, he clicked on the link that held all our moments, precious moments of the past months.

The photos turned around so good and as we clicked through the pictures, I got an idea and told Aaron, "Bee, should we make a night out of it with our family? We can invite them all here and go through these photos with them."

"That's a really good idea. Meekha is also visiting."

"Yes, let's invite them over. Should we do it tonight?" I asked to which Aaron nodded yes and I quickly sent a message to our family chat, and everyone was excited about it.

Soon enough our home was filled with our loved ones. Our parents were busy talking with each other when Meekha and her husband arrived followed by Rianne and Sara.

All of us settled in looking at the photos and reminiscing about those days all over again. We laughed at some funny moments, became emotional at few and I appreciated all those moments frozen in time and the moment that we were sitting together laughing and crying together.

Looking back at our wedding and honeymoon, I realized how much it had taught me about love, family, and relationships. It reminded me of the importance of cherishing the moments we share with our loved ones and appreciating the people who make our lives special. It was a beautiful beginning to our journey together, and I knew that we had a lifetime of love and happiness ahead of us. The moment we shared our vows at the beach, the moment we cast those two stones onto the sea promising each other's company in life's every up and down, the moment, he put the vermillion on my forehead, the moment we exchanged our vows and rings, all these moments I would keep safely in my memories. These moments were also the times in my life when it hit me the most with the realization of getting to spend my life with the person I loved, and the happy tears made their way to my eyes.

We were now starting a new journey of our life filled with its unique ups and downs; helping each other grow in each other's embrace. I will be treasuring these moments with him from now till forever.

THE END

About Author

Jenisha Manandhar was born and raised amidst the vibrant cultural tapestry of Kathmandu, Nepal, where she discovered her passion for storytelling at a young age. With an insatiable imagination and a deep appreciation for the power of words, she embarked on a journey to share her unique narratives with the world. Jenisha Manandhar is a Nepalese writer who believes in the transformative power of literature. Her debut novel, Lost Letters, explores the power of love in the face of adversity. With her multicultural background and a keen eye for human emotions, she crafts narratives that resonate on a universal level. Currently residing in Sydney, Jenisha draws inspiration from the vibrant cityscape and diverse communities around her.

Books by Jenisha Manandhar

Lost Letters

Moving Forward

Acknowledgements

I am deeply grateful for the moments of life that had brought us here together and that had led for me to write this book.

The one reading this book, I wonder what must have motivated you to pick this book out of vast array of books at your disposal. Nevertheless, I am grateful that you gave this book a chance to be part of your reading journey. I hugely appreciate the time and attention you bestowed onto this book. I hope it managed to entertain you and satisfy you. Thank you so much for your support.

My Love, when I first attempted to write a novel, my self-doubt had many times blindsided me and blocked the creation of words in my mind. In each of that moment, my dearest love of my life, my husband, you have helped me get over it by encouraging me and listening to my insane ideas in the middle of the night. Thank you, my love, for always being there for me and having faith in in my stories even when I didn't myself. Thank you for everything you do for me- from listening to my half-baked story to my first completed draft of the story, helping with cover design, and brainstorming with me. I owe it all it you, my love.

My darling mother dearest, I guess I got the penchant of storytelling from you. I am not as good as you are with your poems and words, but I try. I always appreciate your insight for my work and your well-versed motivation to continue writing. From helping me with book launch in Nepal and to talking with distributors, who needs the PR agent, when I have got you. I am grateful to have someone like you as my mother.

My dearest father, on whose eyes, I see the proud glimmer, thank you for always encouraging with the right words and believing in my dreams- supporting them no matter what. I have always appreciated the way you believed in me and told me I could pursue whatever dream I chose.

My family that I was born to and the family that has welcomed me with open arms, thank you so much for your love, patience, and belief in my dreams. Your constant support and the belief you have in me always puts me at awe of how lucky I am to be part of this wholesome, incredible big family. Thank you for encouraging me and being curious of what I would write next.

To the family I made in this beautiful city, Sydney, thank you for the love and support you have bestowed on me throughout these years. Thank you for helping me with the shenanigans I put you through for the promotion of my books. The way my books made it to your bookshelf, the way you read, the way you ask me about my stories and motivate me to write them- I deeply appreciate it. You have been a pillar of strength to me.

Risaa and Shiwani, you are the most amazing girlfriends a girl can ask for. The thoughts you lend me through your words when you went through a chapter I shared, it would be my treasured memories. I really appreciate your input. I love you guys so much for it.

I had the opportunity of having the most amazing, talented women in the field of literature and leading women from different government sectors of Nepal, to grace the book launch event of Lost Letters. Literary Writer Indira Prasai, Poet Usha Sherchan, Deputy Speaker of House of Representatives of Nepal Indira Rana Magar, Deputy Mayor of Kathmandu Metropolitan City Sunita Dangol, Deputy Mayor of Budhanilkantha Municipality Anita Lama, Member of Parliament Yamuna Shrestha, thank you so much for your warm presence and beautiful words of encouragement. All of you being the part of the event was the highlight of my career as an author so far. Thank you so much.

And Sydney the city I have fallen in love with. The city that helped me find the lost me. Thank you.

For my imagination to soar and come in form of words to tell a story, I have you all to thank for. I am deeply grateful for your unwavering support and encouragement.

Gratefully,

Jenisha M